Randi fought  ⟩ght
evaporated into th her
eyes and, for a mo out.
Her eyes hadn't de was
actually here.

But this wasn't the skinny young man who had gone on that mission trip. Now, his body was fuller, broader. He was the same height, all six-foot-two of him, and his hair was the same sable color she remembered. Memories of his touch, his kisses, the love radiating from his deep blue eyes, assaulted her.

The Wade Malone she'd known had been kind, caring, loved life and always had a smile on his face. He loved people and would do anything to help them. That wasn't the man who stood in her yard. This man looked at her with a surprised recognition, then just as quickly, disgust, if not outright hate.

A whimper welled up in her throat.

How could he be the same man who'd left her? The man she'd known had professed his undying love, yet had never returned. Had he found another woman and made his home in Columbia? Did he have children? *Other* children, her heart whispered.

The urge to run to him was tempered by his hard expression, the thin set of his lips. He had no idea of what she'd been forced to live through. Did he even care?

Shattered Promises

by

Linda Trout

Rock Ledge Series

Shattered Promises

Cover Art by *Rae Monet, Inc.*

The Wild Rose Press, Inc.
PO Box 708
Adams Basin, NY 14410-0708
Visit us at www.thewildrosepress.com

Publishing History
First Edition, 2022
Trade Paperback ISBN 978-1-5092-4410-2
Digital ISBN 978-1-5092-4411-9

Rock Ledge Series
Published in the United States of America

Dedication

To every author who has taken the time to encourage other writers to pursue their dreams, giving a hand-up in the process. Your inspirations show that it can, indeed, be done.

To the man of my dreams and my real-life hero, my husband, who continues to support me in all of my endeavors. I will always love you.

Chapter One

Randi Johnson didn't think of herself as a recluse, but enjoyed the solitude of her remote home on forty acres in the Ozark Mountains more than she should. Today, fog so dense it reminded her of pea soup blanketed the area. About to settle down at the kitchen table with her morning coffee, she stopped when she heard an unusual low rumble. It became louder, shaking the dishes in the cabinets and the pictures danced on the walls. Her first thought was an earthquake. Except, they'd never had one in this region before.

She ran onto the porch as the roaring became louder. Was that a plane? If so, it sounded as if it were going to hit her house. Paralyzed with indecision, she was about to move—to where she didn't know—when a mid-sized plane emerged from the fog as it plummeted from the sky. It would miss her home, but was so close she felt as if she could reach out and touch it…and saw the panic on the pilots' faces.

As if in slow motion, she watched in horror as it ripped apart newly leafed out blackjack oak trees, shearing off pieces of the plane as it went. Then the ground shook with the impact, following closely by a deafening explosion.

"Nooo!"

****

It had only been a couple of hours since the plane

had gone down… since Randi's peaceful mountainside had erupted into chaos. Fog dipped and swirled around her as she sat huddled in her old work jacket. Morbid as it was, she couldn't stop watching the activity from the safety of her front porch. Rescue workers moved in and out of view, trying to find survivors of the downed commuter plane. Rock Ledge, Arkansas, a small rural town, wasn't equipped to handle this type of disaster. It wouldn't have mattered how big the town was though, or what type of equipment they had…no one survived.

She knew because she'd looked, had tried to help. But it had been fruitless.

Now, she didn't think she'd ever get the smell of diesel fuel—or burned flesh—out of her nostrils. Tears slid down her cheeks. Even with her eyes closed, the horrific images still assaulted her. No matter how hard she tried, she couldn't erase what she'd seen at the crash site earlier. Nor could she forget the awful ringing in her ears when the plane exploded. She'd expected to hear a lot of noise afterward; yet it'd been eerily quiet. Deathly quiet. The only sound had been the crackling fire burning portions of the plane and surrounding undergrowth.

On the step beside her lay a sooty and dirt covered baby doll. Why she'd picked it up at the crash site was beyond her. Except as a reminder of how fragile life was, of the life of a little girl who would never grow old enough to have children of her own. Randi brushed a bit more dirt off and made a mental note to give the doll to the authorities later so it could be returned to the child's family. Or did all of the immediate family perish on the plane? Bile churned in her stomach at the thought.

Another large truck arrived. This time, men with chainsaws emerged, then began cutting and clearing a way to the wreckage. They hadn't asked permission and they didn't need it. Whatever they needed to do was fine by her...anything to get the debris off her property.

The older farmhouse wasn't much to look at, but it was hers, free and clear. Over the years, she'd made some improvements inside and had enlarged the back deck, but overall, it still looked much the same as the day her grandmother had died and left it to her.

Fumbling for a tissue in her pocket, Randi swiped tears away and blew her nose. Moisture from the porch step seeped through her jeans, chilling her further. The deep fog had thickened during the early April morning, making the entire scene surreal, but now it lifted a little, allowing her to see people moving around more clearly. Then one man in particular caught her eye. His easy gait and carriage as he headed toward the crash site reminded her of someone.

Randi straightened. She blinked and strained for a better view, then sucked in a ragged breath. He looked like... No. It couldn't be. Wade Malone. The only man she'd ever loved, yet who had chosen to walk out of her life.

A shiver of apprehension pricked at her as she peered intently, trying to get a better look at him. But the fog swirled up to obscure his face. Then he was gone–enveloped into the density from which he had emerged. Just as he'd disappeared nine years earlier. He'd left on a peace mission to Columbia, promising to come back to her. Only he never had. A month later she'd discovered a new, more personal issue to deal with. One that wouldn't—couldn't—wait for his return.

Randi pressed the palms of her hands against her eyes. *It's an illusion. It's not him. You* know *it's not him!* Her stomach twisted in knots even as she yearned for the ghost from her past. While in his arms she'd always been warm, loved and, most importantly, safe. But that was before. If only he hadn't gone. If only…

Stop it. You can't turn back the clock. Wishing for Wade to magically reappear, to hold her, to lovingly kiss her again, was asking the impossible. Even as she chastised herself, she pushed off the damp porch as if in a daze and followed the figure into the soupy moisture.

At the edge of her yard, she stopped and a shudder ran through her. Even though she wanted to know who the man was, she couldn't force herself to go farther, to take one more step toward the disaster just out of view. As if in slow motion, she turned and trudged back to the house, to her safe haven.

****

FBI Special Agent Wade Malone had made good time getting to the crash scene, especially taking into account the dangerous fog blanketing the immediate area. He had flown into Harrison, where, thankfully, the fog wasn't as much of a problem. He had to admit, though, he'd been more than a little apprehensive about flying considering another plane had gone down, probably in part due to the limited visibility. Had that been the only reason? Or were other factors involved?

Driving along the winding two-lane highway, he missed the turnoff to the side road and had to find a place to turn around, then finally pulled down the long drive. Various vehicles clogged the single lane dirt road, including a couple of firetrucks with hoses stretched into the trees toward the wreckage. It appeared as if they had been able to contain the fire before the entire forest went up in flames. It surprised Wade how close to the road the wreckage was.

Forced to go farther down the private drive, he passed the initial point of impact where the plane first hit the tree line, and where several men were working with chainsaws to clear a path. When he found a spot to park, he realized it was someone's yard. He could make out a house across the way, but not much else.

He changed from his regular shoes to boots, then shrugged into his FBI jacket and walked back toward the wreckage site, following the path the plane had taken. Once he'd entered the tree line, the rocky terrain made it difficult to get around, and debris from the plane hung suspended from the thick foliage. Normally, he compartmentalized these situations. Despite what most of his coworkers thought, he wasn't heartless, just able to keep his emotions under lock and key. That was what made him so good at his job. It made him able to see his assignments with cold clarity.

He couldn't do that this time, though. Bile clogged his throat. He did *not* want to go down there! He did *not* want to see what he was about to see. It was bad enough all on board were dead, but he had to find his best friend, Eric Logan, and identify his body. He refused to let anyone else do it. Wade owed it to Eric…owed it to his wife, Julie, and their three kids.

Multiple people were milling around and he managed to skirt them, not ready to talk. Actually, he wasn't sure he *could* talk at this point.

Moving over the rough terrain was slow going and he was glad for his foresight in footwear. At times, the only way he knew he was still going in the right direction was from damage to the trees. That and parts of the aircraft littered the area. The fog was thick enough to obscure most of the damage from the planes impact, but he knew there would also be debris from luggage scattered around. Personal items of those onboard. Items of lives and families torn apart.

Stench from jet fuel and burned bodies reached him long before he came upon the actual wreckage, and it threw him back into the jungle from years ago. Nightmarish images slammed into him and he had to stop before he stumbled. He used a tree for support. Clenching his teeth, he closed his eyes and forced that year from his mind. Normally, he controlled his emotions and remained detached, even when working this sort of situation. But none of the other situations involved his best friend. Taking a deep breath, he straightened and moved on.

When he finally arrived at what was left of the fuselage, he was relieved to see the fire from the plane, as well as the surrounding forest, had mostly been put out, though there was an area of brush still burning. The local fire department was spraying it down now. The back portion of the plane was still fairly intact. He'd gotten the passenger manifest before leaving Kansas City and knew where Eric had been sitting. Another marshal had also been on the plane, but was farther up in an area that had been ripped apart. Wade had never met the man and would leave identifying his body to others. Right now, his focus was on his friend.

A few of the workers looked at him curiously as he approached, but they were too busy collecting bodies, and body parts, to pay him much attention. He stepped inside the plane through the gaping hole. At least this

6

portion hadn't burned. Keeping his eyes focused upward as much as possible, he tried his best to not look at the people still strapped in their seats, at the look of shock and terror frozen on their faces. Of the brokenness surrounding all of them. Slowly, he made his way to Eric's seat.

Wade almost doubled over at the sight of his friend. If it weren't for the odd angle in which his head hung, he'd look as if were simply sleeping. Squatting, Wade touched his hand. The hand he had shaken so many times, the hand that had slapped Wade on the back after they'd done a good job, or simply to give him a hard time when Eric had played a joke on him. The hand that had lovingly cupped his wife's face before kissing her in front of everyone at the departmental picnic when she'd announced she was pregnant with their second child.

The hand that was now cold with rigor mortis.

Wade openly wept. For long minutes he allowed his normally contained emotions to wash over him, allowed himself to grieve for his friend. No one bothered him. Each person there felt the magnitude of the lives lost. Finally, he took in huge gulps of air, wiped his eyes, and stood. The dangling open handcuff from Eric's left wrist a reminder of why he'd been on the plane to begin with. A simple prisoner transport. Something he had done multiple times. Only this time had been Eric's final one.

One last deep breath, one last long look at his friend, then, "Don't worry, buddy. I'll take care of Julie and the kids. I'll look after them."

He turned and made his way out of the fuselage, knowing Eric's body would soon be transported, along with all the others. He intended to be one of the men moving him, but first, there were other things to attend to. Wade gulped down another lump in his throat.

Reeling in the emotions, he went in search of the lead investigator with the National Transportation Safety Board. He found Henry Webster, a stocky, balding man with an unlit cigar stuck between his teeth. Wade had worked with him in the past. "Webster."

"Malone," Henry said as the two men shook hands. "Got the call from your office. You got here quick."

"Yeah." He swallowed hard and forced the word out through his tight throat.

"I've informed my people you'll be on-site, so you shouldn't have any trouble. Sorry about the marshals."

He took a deep breath to gather himself. "Thanks. Any theories on the cause of the crash?" Any specific reason why everyone on board had to die?

"Not yet, but according to the eyewitness, it was in one piece before impact so it doesn't sound like a bomb. We'll know more once we locate the black box and the cockpit voice recorder."

Wade nodded, then turned his back on the grisly scene. It'd be a long time before he got the images out of his mind, especially of Eric. "I understand the prisoner they were escorting managed to survive the crash and escaped, but was later taken down."

Webster grunted. "Yeah. Took a woman hostage and the sheriff was forced to shoot him."

Good. He was dead. "That solves that problem."

"Reckon so."

He forced his mind back on track, wanting to know as much as possible about the crash. "Can someone direct me to the eyewitness?"

"Sure. The sheriff can take care of that. His name's Jake Bennett." Webster described what he looked like and wore.

They fell silent as two grim faced men carrying a stretcher passed nearby, then eerily faded ghost-like into the enveloping moisture. "Where are they taking the bodies?"

"A makeshift morgue's been set up in a warehouse in town. Besides the school gym, it's the only place large enough." Henry stuck the cigar back in his mouth and walked away, leaving Wade to stare after him.

Suddenly, the hairs on the back of his neck stood up, but he couldn't pinpoint the reason. He never ignored those twitches, though. Not paying attention could prove fatal.

Numerous people who shouldn't be there moved around the area. Among the FAA, NTSB and local firefighters were the media, and he even spotted a few scavengers darting in and out of the swirling mist. Who, besides scum of the earth, would want a souvenir of a plane crash? Anger pulsed through him at the thought of anyone touching anything of Eric's. But, as much as he'd like to, he couldn't stand over the body until it had been removed.

Still, he had this eerie feeling that had nothing to do with the swirling fog. He glanced around the area again, searching for the source of his unease. Not seeing anything that sent up any major red flags, he turned away, intent on finding the sheriff and the eyewitness.

****

After so many years behind bars, even the acrid stench of jet fuel smelled sweet to Phillip Fry. His release from prison close to a month ago still felt as if it had been yesterday and he relished every minute, every second of being out in the open again. Except his well-oiled plans for a jewelry heist had gone up in flames. Literally. His old cell mate, who was a safe cracker was being transported on the commuter plane. Phillip had worked it all out, how he'd free the man once the plane landed. So he was nearby when he heard the news about the crash and had gotten to the site before it was cordoned off. He had to see for himself that his buddy was really dead.

Wandering around the site, as if he were a photojournalist, he looked twice when a familiar figure came out of the remains of the downed plane. Wade Malone. Phillip stood and stared. He'd been looking for Malone for years. While in the joint, he'd tried his best to track the federal agent, and his career, on the Internet. It had been the only thing that had gotten Phillip through the endless days while he served his time. He'd forced himself to be a model prisoner, and had been released six months early for good behavior, while all he'd wanted to do the entire time he was inside was punch anyone who came near him. It infuriated him that his brother—the only family he had left—was rotting in the ground while Malone still lived.

Now, here he was, a few feet away. Things couldn't have worked out better.

Phillip could've easily shot him, disappeared into the fog, and not been caught. But that would have been too easy. The damn fed was going to suffer first. And he sure as hell would know why he was dying.

Phillip blended in with the reporters canvassing the site, snapping pictures as he went, and watched while his target spoke with someone from the NTSB.

I don't know how yet, but I'll find a way to make you pay. You think you're so good. But you won't figure it out. Not before it's too late. Turning his back as Malone looked around, he smiled to himself. *Yes, this will be sweet revenge. Now I'll watch the agony on your face as you die. Just as you watched the agony on my brother's.*

****

From Webster's description, Wade soon found the sheriff. A few years older than himself, Bennett was close to his own height, with dark hair that was a little too long. Stepping in front of the man, he flashed his badge. "Sheriff, I'm Special Agent Wade Malone with the FBI. Do you have a moment?"

Bennett gave him a quick once over, sizing him up, then extended his hand. "What can I do for you, Agent Malone? You're here because of the marshals who died on the plane?"

"Yes." He wouldn't tell Bennett how long he and Eric Logan had been friends, of the countless hours he'd spent at Logan's house grilling steaks and burgers, having a beer or two, and playing with the kids. Appreciating his friend's happy marriage and normal life. Eric's absence would stay with Wade for years to come.

The sheriff briefly narrowed his eyes at the curt tone in Wade's response. Having members of local law enforcement irritated with him was nothing new to Wade. He didn't care, as long as they cooperated. Usually, it worked better if they *were* a little intimidated. Kept them on their toes and off his back.

But Bennett didn't look intimidated. He had a hard

look about him that indicated he'd been around a while and knew the score. Good. He'd be an asset.

"You interreacted with the escaped prisoner. What can you tell me?"

Bennett's face hardened. "I don't have much on him, except he was pretty banged up when he took a woman hostage and threatened to kill her."

"Was it the homeowner? How did he get inside?" People should lock their doors.

"It wasn't the homeowner. It was… It was the owner of the café who had come out with me to show me the way. I'm new to town and the two women are friends." Bennett looked away as pain flashed across his face. "I thought she'd be okay to walk to the house by herself after I parked down the road. I was wrong."

Ah. Now Wade had a better picture of what had transpired. "But you were able to take him down without harm coming to her. Did he say anything beforehand about the crash?"

Bennett shook his head. "No. He just demanded transportation out of here. Then he became desperate when he realized it wasn't going to happen. I had to keep her safe so took the shot."

He nodded, understanding the other man's feelings. "Not something you wanted to do."

Bennett grimaced. "Hate taking another's life, but would do it again in a heartbeat."

"Hazard of the job." He didn't know yet if Eric had died in the crash, or if the fugitive had managed to kill him. If the latter, Wade wished he'd been the one to end the scum bag's life. "It still isn't easy."

"Nope."

Dealing with death was simply part of the job.

Didn't mean they had to like it, but they each did what they had to do. Time to change the subject. "Were you the first to arrive at the crash scene this morning?" Wade opened a small notebook.

"No. That was the homeowner, Randi Johnson, and then my deputy."

"And where is Johnson now?"

"Inside. But this might not be—"

"Now is fine. Lead the way." Bennett scowled at the sudden shift in his demeanor. He didn't blame the sheriff. Wade's *style* of investigating was pretty off-putting, but it got the job done. The sheriff gave a slight nod, turned and headed in the direction he'd come from.

Wade fell into step beside him. No questions, just simple compliance. Good, because Wade had developed respect for the man and, despite Wade's usual lack of caring for others' opinions, didn't want to be on Bennett's bad side.

At the house, Wade stayed on the lawn as Bennett climbed the porch steps and knocked. He spoke with the homeowner, then waited until Johnson handed him something. A moment later he turned and dipped his head; his jaw clenched, his lips pressed into a tight line and turned down. He swallowed before he blew out a hard breath. Clutched in his hand was a child's doll. A dirty doll. It only took Wade a gut-wrenching breath to realize where the toy had come from, and what it represented.

Damn. Wade hated tragedies like this where families were torn apart...or totally destroyed. He hadn't seen a child in the section of the plane he'd been in. That meant the child and her parents had been in a section that had been totally destroyed. The thought of the little girl and what had happened to her tugged at him. Like Bennett, he swallowed hard.

Then Bennett stepped aside, giving Wade full view of the owner.

Every muscle in his body froze before a tremor shook him to his core. *Miranda Seavers.* A lightning bolt hitting him in the solar plexus wouldn't have shocked him more. Too stunned to say anything, he just stood there, soaking in her beauty. Seeing her was like a five-course dinner to a starving man…enticing, alluring. Her auburn hair emphasized her ivory skin and sea green eyes. She was fuller, softer. Her denim jeans clung to the long legs that made up her five-foot eight-inch frame.

But seeing her was also like one of the torture devices used on him while a captive in the jungle. He felt as if he'd walked over a bed of hot coals to find nothing but a cliff at the end and no way of going back. She'd lied to him, turned her back the minute he was on the plane to Columbia. When he'd finally returned to the States and had gone to her house, she wasn't there. Instead, she'd gone to Dallas, according to her mom, who seemed to gain immense pleasure in telling him he wasn't wanted there and never had been. She said Miranda had been stringing him along.

Once Mrs. Seavers had put him in his place, and with a smug expression, she had slammed the door in his face. Crushed, he vowed he'd be like Miranda and simply walk away, to not think of her again. Only his heart wouldn't listen. For months, she had been his emotional lifeline of trying to simply survive from one day to the next. He couldn't turn off his love like flipping a switch. Not initially, anyway.

Once he'd joined the FBI, he'd looked in every database he could discretely access. Nothing. It was as if she'd dropped off the planet. If she'd changed her name, he hadn't found it. Finally, he'd given up. Miranda did not want to be found. He learned to bury her memory, to bury his love for her and construct a steel vault around his heart, forever blocking her out. He'd been unable to have any sort of meaningful relationship with anyone else since. There had been nothing left in him to give. Now, he just didn't care.

At least he hadn't thought so until a few seconds ago.

Then she looked at him, her face pale and drawn. As they stood there, neither said a word. What was going through her mind? Finally, the sheriff's voice penetrated his senses.

"Ms. Johnson, you don't have to do this right now if you're not up to it."

She swayed and Bennett took her arm to steady her. "Wade," she whispered.

"Miranda." Wade had a hard time saying her name, and it came out more of a guttural growl.

Then it apparently struck the sheriff. "You two know each other?"

"Yes."

"No," Wade said at the same time. Finding her here, a short distance from his dead friend, was worse than being poked with a cattle prod, something he'd endured many times. For the briefest of moments, he wished he was back in the jungle. Back to when he believed she loved him and was waiting for him. He'd overcome that fantasy long ago. Looking at her now, he

15

almost felt sorry for her and what she'd seen that morning. But he refused to be moved by her presence. Reaching deep, he locked the memories of their past away.

Only not quite quick enough.

The flood of images of them together, of her tender caresses, of her kisses, threatened to bring him to his knees. Unable to look at her any longer, he turned and walked away, forcing his stiff legs to move at a steady pace, forcing his lungs to function at a normal level. Forcing his brain to block out the emotional turmoil his heart had suffered. He refused to look back despite every cell in his body demanded he do so, even when she called his name.

After all these years, when he's sent to investigate a plane crash, he finds her standing there. Not Miranda Seavers, but Randi Johnson. No wonder he'd been unable to find her. The question was, why did she change her name? Or had she gotten married? He hadn't found any evidence of a marriage license, but that didn't necessarily mean it hadn't happened. Did he really want to know? A tiny part of him said yes, while every other fiber of his being shouted a resounding *no*.

He'd have to talk to her at some point. But not now. He needed space to get his emotions under control, to make sure his heart was securely closed off so he could do the job he was sent here to do. Hopefully, the investigation wouldn't take too long. Then he'd leave and go on with his life.

Without her.

Just like he'd done for years.

Chapter Two

Randi fought for breath as all coherent thought evaporated into thin air. Black dots danced before her eyes and, for a moment, she thought she might pass out. Her eyes hadn't deceived her earlier. Wade Malone was actually here.

But this wasn't the skinny young man who had gone on that mission trip. Now, his body was fuller, broader. He was the same height, all six-foot-two of him, and his hair was the same sable color she remembered. Memories of his touch, his kisses, the love radiating from his deep blue eyes, assaulted her.

The Wade Malone she'd known had been kind, caring, loved life and always had a smile on his face. He loved people and would do anything to help them. That wasn't the man who stood in her yard. This man looked at her with a surprised recognition, then just as quickly, disgust, if not outright hate.

A whimper welled up in her throat.

How could he be the same man who'd left her? The man she'd known had professed his undying love, yet had never returned. Had he found another woman and made his home in Columbia? Did he have children? *Other* children, her heart whispered.

The urge to run to him was tempered by his hard expression and the thin set of his lips. He had no idea of what she'd been forced to live through. Did he even care?

Shunned by her overly zealous and fanatically religious parents, Randi had been forced out on her own. At nineteen, she'd been naïve and had struggled until a kind soul had pointed her toward an organization that helped unwed teen mothers. In the end, she'd given up her baby.

All because he'd misled her. Had his lies simply been to sleep with her before he left? Would he have come back if he'd known she was pregnant? All the months of hoping to see him again, to have him rescue her so she wouldn't have to give away their child still taunted her dreams.

Where were you when I needed you most? she wanted to shout in his face.

Too shocked to say anything, she was stunned when Wade ignored her, pivoted and walked away. No hello, how are you.

No explanation of where he'd been all these years.

She barely registered the sheriff as he also left without a word. Stealing a look at Wade's retreating back, she staggered inside the house, locked the door and slid to the floor.

It had taken her years to get over him. After giving birth to their child, she'd come to Rock Ledge to care for her sick maternal grandmother. Then, after Granny Woods' death, Randi had inherited the house and property. Since her parents had made it abundantly clear she wasn't welcome back in Tulsa, she'd gladly stayed. She'd relished the seclusion and the bittersweet memories made with Granny. She'd healed here, made a place for herself.

But after seeing Wade for the first time in years, she felt truly alone. Despair threatened to overwhelm her until Sebastian, her overweight cat, climbed into her lap. She automatically scratched between his ears, his favorite place besides his belly. His loud purr made her smile.

"If I thought it'd do any good, I'd put you on a diet." She laughed at him as she adjusted him more evenly across her lap while she stretched her legs out. A Russian Blue, he was unusually large. She'd rescued him from the animal shelter when his previous owner didn't want him. "Too big" and "eats too much," the woman had said.

"I got the better end of that deal, didn't I?" She lovingly scratched his back with long, gentle motions. The other woman's junk was Randi's treasure. His constant purring relaxed her, pushing the morning's events to the back of her mind.

After the cat had gotten his fill of attention, he jumped off her lap, then proceeded to pad to the kitchen and his water bowl. "Rotten cat," she muttered. Despite his being so spoiled, Randi wouldn't trade him for the world.

She stood and stretched the kinks from her back. How long would it take to clean up the wreckage? How long would all the people be around? She loved the solitude and remoteness of her home, but for the time being it was a beehive of activity.

Even though the forest would eventually reclaim the charred and broken land, Randi didn't want a constant reminder of what had happened staring her in the face every time she walked out her front door. As soon as possible, she'd have plants, shrubs and trees planted to camouflage the makeshift road they were building. Still, she didn't think she'd ever recover from what she had seen.

She started thinking of the best way to honor those whose lives had been lost. Making a permanent shrine wasn't something she wanted to do. That would only encourage people to return here again and again. Holding a memorial for the families after the cleanup was done, though, would be something she'd be more than willing to host. If she'd lost someone on the plane, morbid as it was, she'd want to visit the site where they died—to be able to say goodbye to their spirit there.

And then there was Wade. Somehow, she'd have to find a way of dealing with her emotions…and him.

Still restless, she gravitated to her work room, Sebastian trailing behind. He made one circle around the room to ensure his favorite toys were still where they were supposed to be, then he jumped into the window bed she'd placed there for him. While he preened himself, she put a clean canvas on the easel and set out her brushes. Painting always took her mind off anything bothering her. Hopefully, today would be no different.

Granny had recognized her talent and encouraged her, going so far as to give up her sewing room, located on the southwest corner of the house, so Randi could pursue her painting career. A portrait of the two of them hung close to her workstation. Randi had painted it from a picture taken before Granny's health became critical. Both smiling and sitting in a swing glider in the yard, her friend, Melody Rose, had snapped the picture at sunset one summer day.

Brilliant red and yellows in the sky, along with

deep purple clouds, served as a backdrop of the lush oak trees surrounding the house. Randi had on cut-offs and a tattered t-shirt, and Granny wore one of her old work dresses, her favorite orange sweater draped over her shoulders. They had been working in the flower beds but had stopped for a break when Melody had shown up. Glasses of iced tea sat on the arms of the glider, and Granny's yellow straw hat lay on the ground at her feet.

Even now, the picture gave her comfort and peace.

Randi squirted several colors of paint on the palette, picked up her brush and started painting. No thought as to what she was creating, she let go and allowed her emotions to guide her without truly seeing what she was doing. In the past, this method had created some of her best work.

As the morning wore on, her muscles stiffened and cramped, and her breathing became shallow. She blinked, then stood back and stared at the canvas, horrified. The image glaring at her reflected the destruction she'd seen earlier. She hadn't painted any bodies, just nondescript blobs where she assumed people had lain. The picture was all black and gray with red and yellow flames against a background of charred, leafless trees. Her gaze drifted to a small white shape in the lower right-hand corner and she had to look closely to see what it was. Her hand started to shake. The baby-doll she'd retrieved, then given to the sheriff, was the only light on the canvas.

Unable to look at the image any longer, she hurriedly cleaned the brushes and left the room, closing the door behind her. She was thankful Sebastian hadn't been locked inside and now lay sprawled in the middle of the hallway. She fervently needed to wash the picture out of her mind. After a quick shower, she dressed in khakis and a lightweight top. The sun had finally burned off the fog and turned the day warm. She headed into the kitchen, but stopped at a sound outside the back door. She peeked out the window, then breathed a sigh of relief to see Melody dumping ice into a large tub filled with bottled water.

Randi threw open the door and hugged her. "You're back." Her best friend had had her own trauma that morning. As soon as she'd heard about the downed plane, she had come running to check on Randi. Mel had been taken at gunpoint by the only person to survive the crash—a criminal being escorted by a US Marshal. Sheriff Bennett had shot and killed him, saving Melody's life. Both women had held each other and cried over their respective stories before Mel had gone back to town. She needed to check on her café, The Tangled Rose.

Melody emptied another bag of ice into the tub. "Yeah. I brought food for the rescue workers. We just need to get it set out."

"I hadn't even thought of them being hungry." Randi's mind had been elsewhere.

"All the churches in town pitched in to help. They're restricting the people at the crash site, so everyone dropped their food off at the café and I brought it out. I hope you don't mind." The dark circles under Melody's eyes were a stark testament to what she'd endured earlier.

Grateful for the diversion, Randi helped drag a couple of long folding tables out of the garage and set them up on the large, and thankfully shaded, back porch. Randi had enlarged and covered the porch last year and it was the perfect place to enjoy her morning coffee or meals. The gently sloping ground gave the appearance of a much taller porch than it actually was. With the sandwiches, huge bowls of potato salad, baked beans, coleslaw, chips and an assortment of cookies, brownies and cupcakes in place, she flagged down the first worker she saw and told him to spread the word.

Within minutes, recovery workers were coming around the side of the house.

Randi shouldn't have been shocked at how dirty they were, but was taken aback, anyway. "Would you like to come inside and wash up?" she asked the first person to arrive.

"No, ma'am. But we'd be much obliged if we could use your water hose. That'll be good enough."

"Of course. Please. Help yourself." She hurried inside and came back out with a new bar of soap and a couple rolls of paper towels. She was grateful Port-a-Potties had already been set up close to the crash site.

After each person had washed and stepped up onto the porch, without fail, each one expressed their gratitude for the food. As far as she knew, none of them had eaten since they had arrived. They came in small groups, filled their plates and ate under the trees in the yard. Once they left, another group showed up. Work at the crash site never stopped.

The sheriff showed up half an hour after they started serving. She noticed Mel stiffened when he stood in front of her, tension sizzling between them. But it was no surprise after what had happened earlier. Since Mel had witnessed her husband's murder a couple years ago, Randi couldn't imagine how she was holding up so well after having a gun pointed at her this morning. She was one of the strongest women Randi had ever met. Either that, or she was good at masking her feelings. Either way, Randi wished she had some of it because she was having a hard time facing her past.

A past who was walking toward her right now.

Despite his coldness earlier, she was still overwhelmed by seeing Wade again and mentally drank in the sight of his rock-hard body, the way his tousled hair and his scruffy beard made him appear rugged— sexy. No longer wearing his FBI jacket, he was as dirty, and looked as tired, as the others. The man she had known never shirked on any duties, helping anyone who needed assistance. It appeared as if he was still the same way, in that regard, anyway.

He paused at the bottom step and looked up at her, his gaze cutting into her. What was he thinking? Feeling? Finally, he moved to the serving table, acknowledging both ladies with a nod. He kept his head down as he filled his plate.

As he neared the end of the line, he still hadn't said anything to her. She wanted to cry, to scream, or even throw something. But not in front of Melody. Even though they were good friends, some things were still private. This was a part of her past Randi hadn't shared with anyone, and she didn't plan to start now.

Melody took an empty platter into the kitchen, leaving her alone with her thoughts. Should she confront Wade and make him talk to her? Or let it go? Let *them* go? While she debated what to do, he took his food and stepped off the porch, heading back the way he'd come. All reasonable thought left her and she stormed after him. The man was going to talk to her if she had to beat it out of him.

As he reached the edge of the yard, she called his name. He stopped, then slowly turned to face her.

"Are you ever going to speak to me?" she demanded.

He stood there for several heartbeats as sweat ran between her breasts, the hot sun heating her back. His gaze slowly raked her body up and down, then his lip curled up in derision.

With that one gesture, her stomach curdled. She no longer had anything to say to him. Not about the past. Not about today. Without another word, she pivoted and headed back to the house. Randi counted her blessings he hadn't tried to stop her. Or worse, touch her. If he had, she would've gone off like a Roman Candle. Or a plane exploding on impact. Either way, the ending wouldn't have been good.

****

Wade watched as Miranda marched across the yard to the house. He'd sneered at her, as if she were nothing more than a piece of meat. In reality, the sight of her made it hard for him to draw a breath…the past rushing back at him full force. He tucked his chin and clenched his jaw. No, he refused to go down that quagmire of a hole. He'd learned his lesson years ago. She was right about one thing, though, they did need to clear the air. He'd find out why she'd left him, then *he'd* be the one walking away. He'd go back to doing what he did best…catching bad guys. And to do that, he needed to retain his hatred for her. That hatred had fueled him, making him the man he was today—hard, cold.

And damned efficient.

****

Waltz Rite In, the neon sign read. Located on the outskirts of town, the rundown bar looked exactly like Phillip Fry's kind of place. He pushed on the door that was badly in need of a coat of paint and entered the dimly lit beer joint. Stale beer permeated the air as he crossed the less than clean wooden floor, then he took a seat at the bar.

"Whiskey, neat," he told the bartender when the man wandered over.

"You here because of the crash?" the bartender asked after he'd set the drink in front of Phillip.

"Yeah. Photojournalist." Phillip grimaced. "I was out there earlier and it was horrible. I had to get away and wash some of the smoke out of my throat."

The bartender nodded. "Glad you stopped in." With that, he went back to work.

He hadn't asked a lot of questions. Good. Usually, in places like this, they had a tendency to mind their own business.

After watching Malone most of the morning, he still hadn't come up with the perfect plan to kill him. But he would. It was only a matter of time until the right opportunity presented itself. It'd be harder to get back in to the crash site, and close to Malone, but he wasn't worried. In a town this small, he had to be staying at one of the few motels. It'd be easy enough to find out and track him down.

He was roused out of his thoughts by a loud commotion at one of the tables. In fact, it was the only occupied table in the place. The bartender glared at them, but said nothing.

"Hey, buddy. What's with those two?" Phillip nodded toward the pair.

"Ah, just a couple of the locals. Harry, the tall one is a reporter for the town paper. Sounds like he got scooped on the plane story and he ain't happy about it." The bartender pulled a tin cup from behind the bar, spit tobacco juice into it, then shoved the cup back into place.

Intent on getting more information, Phillip ignored the dribble of dark juice clinging to the man's lip. "You don't say. Well, the other guy must be a really good friend to get soused this early with him."

"Yeah, well, it's more like the other way around. The skinny, grungy one is Leo and he's the town drunk. Don't know why they're such good buds. Have been ever since Harry moved here 'bout ten years ago thinking he'd make a name for himself with the newspaper. He did, but not the kind of name he wanted. If you ask me, they're both from the same pig waller."

Phillip didn't answer, just nodded. Actually, he understood far more from their short conversation than the bartender would ever know. A seed had been planted in his mind. A couple of minutes after the other man went into the back, Phillip quietly moved to a table close to the other two and listened to their conversation.

"You telling me you didn't get anywhere close to the plane?" Leo leaned across the table as if his friend couldn't hear him.

Harry took a swig of his beer. "Stupid sheriff. He should know how we do things here. By the time I finally recovered from my hangover and heard about the crash, he already had the Nasty Guard surrounding the place. Said no one was allowed in, not even me!" He slammed his hand down on the table, cursing his poor timing.

"Whose bright idear was it to hire a Yankee sheriff, anyway? We don't need his kind. Why didn't the mayor just make his nephew the new sheriff? Seems easy enough to me."

"Hell if I know. But I heard the town council wanted someone with more experience than Clay. From what I can tell, he's happy to stay a deputy." Harry shook his head. "Man, if I had an opportunity to grab power like that, I'd take it."

Leo slapped him on the back. "You and me both."

Harry hung his head and muttered, "This should've been my chance to move up, maybe even get a better job in Fayetteville."

"Hey! You can't go leaving me. You're the only friend I got."

"You're right, buddy. We gotta stick together." He downed the last of his beer. "We gotta find a way to get even with that sheriff."

Phillip smiled to himself. He had no interest in the sheriff, but these two were the type of men he could use in other ways. His old man had taught him and his younger brother to spot easy marks at an early age, and these two fit the bill perfectly.

"Okay, so whatcha wanna do?" Leo asked.

"Well, I say—first, let's get drunk. Yo, Pete, another round," Harry yelled as he threw his arm in the air to get the bartender's attention, as if they weren't the only ones in the bar.

Except for Phillip.

After Pete brought the next round of beers over, the two men put their heads together, apparently to plan their strategy. Pete ignored their conversation, but Phillip had no intention of letting this opportunity pass.

Keeping his gaze on his own drink, he listened intently.

"Hey, man, whatdaya' think you're doin'?" Harry demanded as he finally noticed him at the nearby table.

"Just sitting here enjoying my drink. That's all," he replied politely.

Still leery, Harry continued to study him a bit longer. Then he saw the expensive camera Phillip had set on the table. "Wow, man. Where'd you get that?"

He didn't know why he'd brought the camera inside, except as part of his cover, but now he was glad. It gave him an opening with the local. "Oh, this? Picked it up not too long ago hoping to get some better pictures." He'd been lucky to find the camera at a pawn shop, thinking it might come in handy. It definitely had this morning.

"It's a Canon, right?" Harry was all but drooling.

"Yeah. An EOS RP. Wish I had've gotten a better one, but this was the best I could do." Or *wanted* to do. The camera served as a prop, nothing else. Right now, it was paying off.

"You a reporter?" Harry asked. He'd turned his chair halfway around, intrigued with the camera, but suspicion still laced his voice.

"Naw, a freelance photographer. It didn't do me any good here, though. Couldn't get within half a mile of the wreckage," he lied. "How about you?"

Harry frowned at him. "What about me?"

"I've heard your name around town as the best reporter they've ever had. Surely they gave you the exclusive on the crash."

"Well, yeah I'm good." He studied him a while, then said, "But that new sheriff only let the national people in there."

Phillip raised his eyebrows in mock surprise. The same sheriff who had killed his cohort. But that was of no consequence now. Not when Malone was within his sights. "Seriously? You being local could give a much better perspective on the impact the crash has on the community."

Harry studied him a bit longer before letting his guard down, then nodded at him. "You're all right, man."

"Hey! What are ya' doing talkin' to that A-hole for?"

"Shut up, Leo. You're drunk," Harry twisted around to face his friend. Then he turned back. "Sorry, he's pissed for getting thrown in jail the other night when he'd had a little too much to drink. The old sheriff would've let him go on home to sleep it off. Not this guy. Just 'cause Bennett's from up north, he thinks we're all dumb hicks down here."

"Some people like to throw their weight around just because they wear a badge. They don't appreciate the average working stiff like us."

"You can say that again," Leo proclaimed loudly.

Harry frowned at his friend, who was close to being totally drunk, before turning his attention back to Phillip.

"I need to mosey on along," Phillip said after he finished his drink then stood. He picked up the camera, then drew two twenty-dollar bills out of his pocket and dropped them on the table in front of the drunks. "Here, let me buy you boys a round or two."

"What's this for?" Leo scowled at him.

"Not a thing. Just being friendly. Maybe you can do me a favor some time."

"Like what?" Harry asked.

"Oh, I don't know, nothing major. I scratch your back and you scratch mine. That sort of thing."

Harry scooped up the discarded bills. "Sure man. No problem. We're here most nights."

And days, Phillip thought as he strolled out of the bar feeling smug. *It had been a productive stop.* He didn't know how yet, but he was sure the two men inside would come in handy in the near future. Very handy indeed.

Chapter Three

Late in the day, Wade stepped inside his room at the Swiss Alps Motel, grateful for the bit of cool air coming from the vent. An older motel, the furnishings were a bit worn, but the place was clean. He wouldn't complain...he had a room. The workers at the crash site ate and slept there until the job was done. Of course, once the hordes of news media had descended upon the town, every available room had been snatched up.

Covered in dirt and sweat, he longed for a shower and wondered if he'd ever get the smell of burnt flesh out of his nostrils. Or the smell of jet fuel. He hated assignments like this, especially when it involved a close friend. The only good he saw was Eric hadn't been burned. Julie would be able to look him in the face before telling him goodbye. He couldn't say the same for the other marshal, and cringed. His wife and kids were faced with a much grimmer funeral.

Permanent goodbyes. Always a possibility of the job, and one they all accepted and faced on a daily basis. Wade wondered why his number had never come up like it had for Eric. Guilt for still being alive slammed into Wade. For all of his dangerous assignments, he had always come out alive. Even in the jungle. Others died, yet he'd lived. Why? What made him so special? Did he have a guardian angel looking over his shoulder? He snorted. Yeah, right. Skill, stubbornness, and he grudgingly admitted, luck, had kept him on the green side of the grass.

He stopped in the middle of the room, closed his eyes and pinched the bridge of his nose. The day's events and images ate at him, especially the sight of Miranda. Shivers ran up his body. Memories of the past—of *their* past—threatened to suck him down a rabbit hole.

Instead of succumbing to the emotion, he blew out a weary breath, then glanced in the mirror over the dresser. It had a large wavy crack running from the upper left corner down to the lower right corner, dividing and distorting his features. "That's what I am, all right, two different people. One the hard, efficient Fed, the other—oh, who knows who the other one is?" he snarled. Disgusted with himself, he headed for the shower.

Refreshed, he came out with a towel draped over his shoulders and another wrapped around his waist. He sank down at the small round table in the corner. His stomach twisted at the loss of his friend and the pain his widow was going through. Wade wished he had been there to tell her, to comfort her, but his skills were better utilized here. Even though others would be with her, he had to talk to her and picked up his phone. The conversation was short, him murmuring his regrets, her stumbling through words as she sobbed.

After they disconnected, he allowed the deep sorrow to wash over him. Tears stung his eyes. Damn but he was going to miss Eric! Wade sat there for a long while, remembering the good times they'd had, how they'd saved each other's lives numerous times. How they had clicked almost from the beginning when they went through the FBI academy together and had hated when Eric had eventually switched to the marshal's office. He had been the only man Wade had felt truly close to. Now he was gone.

Sucking in a deep breath, Wade found the remote control and turned on the flat screen TV attached to the wall. He needed a distraction from the emotions that threatened to overpower him. After flipping through every station and finding nothing that held his interest, he shut it off. The paperwork on the accident needed his attention, anyway, but after spending half an hour looking at it, he hadn't gotten past one single page. He had managed to compartmentalize Eric's death in order to deal with the business at hand, but thoughts of Miranda kept taunting him.

For years, Wade had thought his past was behind him, dead and buried, much like the people he'd gone to South America with. And he'd eventually lumped Miranda into the same category. But finding her here, alive and well, dredged up all the feelings he had mentally buried. Even though he was reluctant to face his past, and without delving deeper into his actions, he quickly dressed and walked out of the room. The unfinished report could wait.

He climbed into his car and headed back to her house. The setting sun in his eyes made the winding road trickier to maneuver, almost as bad as the fog had been that morning.

Noise from the crash site greeted him as he pulled down the drive to Miranda's. Bright floodlights from the scene sent eerie shadows through the trees. The activity wouldn't stop until every last piece of debris, and human remains, had been retrieved. Wade parked in front of the house and turned off the engine. Instead of getting out, he sat there, debating what to say to her. Wondering why in the world he was putting himself through this. Tamping down the jitters that suddenly sprang up, he wrapped mental steel armor around himself, got out of the car and marched up to the porch.

Raising his hand, he hesitated. Had he lost his mind? Probably. Then, resolved to get this over with so he could move on with his life, he knocked. No answer, no movement from inside. He knocked again, louder. Still, the door didn't open. He backed away, ready to leave. Stepping off the front porch he stopped and took a deep breath. Coming here hadn't been a good idea. There wasn't anything for them to say to each other.

Except there was.

Now that he'd found her, he needed to know the truth. The past needed to be settled between them. Perhaps there'd be time tomorrow. He'd taken two steps toward the car when Miranda's voice floated on the air. He walked around the side of the house to the back. The woman he'd once swore he'd love forever sat on a lower porch step, singing to an extremely large cat. Wade stood in the dusky shadows, listening to a song from her childhood, a song he recognized and knew the words to. For a fraction of a second, he almost sang along with her. Then good sense returned and he stepped into the dim porch light.

****

The song had always soothed Randi's soul and tonight was no different. Bless Sebastian for sitting with her...giving her comfort. At least he appeared to like her singing as well as the head scratches she gave him. As the last note faded away, she expected to hear the normal sounds of the forest. Only there weren't any. But they'd be back, once the cleanup was done and all the people and machines were gone, the tree frogs would return. Later, there would be cicadas to add to natures sounds.

"Nice song."

She jumped and swallowed a shriek, then muttered a curse when the hot cocoa she'd been drinking spilled onto her hand. Wade stood a few feet away.

The wind ruffled his sable brown hair, giving him a boyish look that was at odds with his previous demeanor. He wore a blue denim shirt, a pair of tight-fitting jeans and cowboy boots. Instead of a member of the recovery team, he looked like he had grown up in the Ozark Mountains.

As if he had always been here.

She sucked in a ragged breath at the overwhelming tug on her heart. Then she tamped down the emotion. It wouldn't do any good for her thoughts to stray in that direction. Best to keep things in perspective.

"How—how long have you been standing there?" She'd hoped sitting on the back porch, away from the general view of those who might be coming and going from the property, would give her a measure of privacy. Now, with Wade standing so close, she felt exposed.

"Not long." His flat tone didn't give her any indication as to his mood.

As she wiped the cocoa off her hand onto her jeans, she glared at him. "What are you doing here?" *Besides scaring me half to death.*

He moved closer to the porch in slow deliberate steps and stopped a few feet away before he answered.

"Looking for you."

She leaned back, eyeing him cautiously as he simply stood there, staring.

"Think the cat's big enough?" he finally asked as he moved closer, then bent down to scratch Sebastian's head.

That was weird. Sebastian didn't take to strangers, but he rubbed his head on Wade's knuckles, purring like there was no tomorrow.

Wade had been so cold earlier, and now he acted almost civil. Sort of. Her self-defense radar was on full alert. Which was the real Wade Malone? "He's just a big boy." She knew she should cut back on his food, but didn't have the heart to deny him his favorite treats.

Mesmerized, she stared into Wade's eyes, not sure of what she saw in those blue pools, then finally tore her gaze away to concentrate on the woods. Why did he affect her this way? After everything that had happened, all he had to do was get within a hundred feet of her and her stomach immediately tied up in knots.

Even though he wasn't exactly glaring at her right now, she wasn't fooled. His cool reception earlier in the day told her what she needed to know—he didn't have any feelings for her. Not anymore. She hid her emotions before turning to face him again.

"You know what I mean. Is there something you want specifically, or are you just snooping around?" She didn't even try to keep the sharp edge out of her voice.

Propping a booted foot on a porch step, he leaned his arms across his thigh, bringing him eye to eye with her. The position stretched the denim, outlining his muscular thighs. Randi found it hard to keep from ogling his legs. Pulling her gaze back to his, she almost squirmed under his intense stare.

Silence, as thick as the fog had been that morning, stretched between them. Sebastian, oblivious to her discomfort, curled around Wade's leg, begging for more rubbing. Which Wade absently provided.

"Why did you do it, Miranda?" The question was spoken so low she almost didn't hear him.

A bug buzzed around her head, but she ignored it. Swallowing hard, she choked out, "I don't know what you mean."

A low growl emitted from his throat and he leaned forward, placing his face only inches from hers. "Don't play games. Tell me—"

Sebastian let out a screech, then jumped from the porch. His movement knocked Wade backward and a second later the storm door behind them shattered. Before she knew what was happening, Wade threw himself over her, pressing her painfully into the porch steps. Stunned, she couldn't move or form a coherent thought. What in the world? A few seconds passed with him on top of her, unmoving. Heat radiated off his body and for a moment, the last time he'd been on top of her flashed through her mind…the night they'd made love.

Shaking off the image, and ready to tell him to get off and explain why he had assaulted her, he raised up, grabbed her arm and yanked her to her feet. Bending over her, he shoved her toward the house in front of him. He opened the door to the kitchen and pushed her inside, not giving her time to ask what was happening, much less stop and inspect the broken glass laying on the porch.

She whirled around in time to see him pull a gun out of a holster, then throw the deadbolt and turn out the lights.

Standing in silhouette from the light from the living room, she said, "Wade, what do you think you're doing? What's going on?"

"Get down low and turn out the other lights."

"Why? You need to explain yourself." Her back hurt where he'd pressed her into the edge of the steps and she was sure bruises were already forming. When she didn't obey his command, he moved to her and tugged her to the floor. Now she was mad. This was *her* house! How dare he treat her like this? "Listen here—"

"Someone's shooting at us."

She looked at him in disbelief. She opened her mouth. Then closed it again. Her brain was having trouble comprehending the words. "Wh—what?"

"Were you hit? Are you okay?" Concern etched his voice as his hand remained on her arm.

She had to think, and mentally checked her body, though she found it hard to concentrate with him so close...and still touching her. "Uh, no. I don't think I'm hurt." She thought she heard him murmur *thank goodness*, but it was said so quietly, she wasn't sure.

"I need you to turn out the other lights without getting off the floor. Can you do that?"

She nodded and crawled to the living room doorway, reached up and flipped off the lights, plunging the house into darkness. She heard the deadbolt being flipped. Wade had already moved to the back door.

"Wait. Where are you going?" Surely he wasn't going outside. Enough people had died on her property today and she didn't want to add him to the list.

Every instinct she possessed told her he wouldn't stick around, that she'd never see him again after the wreckage had been cleaned up. Part of her mourned that fact, the rest of her was resolved to it. She'd survived on her own all these years, and she'd continue doing so. Wishing for things that could never be was a waste of energy. Despite that, she still worried about his well-being.

"I'm going to check it out."

"But if someone was shooting at us, they might still be out there." Despite her efforts to sound normal, her voice quivered.

"True. Now stay here, lock this door behind me and don't open it for anyone other than me. Do you understand?" His statement was more of a command than a request.

Her heart beat so loud she was sure he heard it from across the room.

"Miranda? Do you understand?" This time his voice was a little gentler.

Sucking in a deep breath, she replied, "Yes. I understand. Is there something I should do while you're gone?"

"Call 9-1-1, but they won't be able to get here before the shooter's gone."

"Unless he's waiting for you to come out the door."

He surprised her and actually chuckled. "There is that. Now move over here so you can lock up."

She did as instructed, crowding his shoulder when she reached his side. With a speed that amazed her, he opened the door and was gone. Quickly flipping the deadbolt behind him, she suppressed the urge to look out the window as he had done. She listened intently, trying to determine where he was. She didn't hear any gunfire. Then again, she hadn't heard any the first time, so there were no guarantees he hadn't been shot the minute he stepped outside.

Her heart continued to beat a fast staccato as she waited. Finally, she remembered to place the call. Brenda, the dispatcher, told her Deputy Larson would be there as soon as possible. Thank goodness Clay was coming. She didn't know the new sheriff and felt comfortable with her motorcycle riding buddy. But would his being here also put him in danger?

****

Phillip cursed. He'd been impulsive and had almost gotten caught. Now the cops would be on high alert, even though it looked as if they were short on manpower. Although, Malone would probably bring in more feds. Damn. Maybe the job Phillip had set out to do wouldn't be finished in the manner he wanted before more cops showed up, after all.

But when he'd seen Malone and the woman so close on the porch, he couldn't pass up the opportunity. He thought he'd timed it right. It would've been perfect if the woman had died in front of him, her head exploding. But who could've guessed the fed would have backed off like he did and screw up the shot? Up until then, they sure looked cozy.

No matter. Malone hadn't seen him when he'd searched the grounds; the trees and darkness had provided adequate cover. He was confident they wouldn't find him, anyway. He was too good.

He quietly made his way back through the woods,

taking a similar route his two new friends had shown him earlier. Good thing because he never would have found a way to the house, and around all the National Guard, without being seen and caught. All it took was a sympathetic ear, some more cash for beer, and a promise to get the two drunks some notoriety. They'd make the headlines all right…after Phillip killed them.

But they might start talking before then. Or bragging. Drunks or not, people might listen. At least once Phillip had his bearings, he'd sent them back to town so they had no idea of what had transpired afterwards.

Unless they heard the news through the grapevine. Small towns were notorious for being gossip mills. Double damn. His bad mood got worse. Then he came across an old barn. He stopped, looked in the direction of the house, then back at the barn. An idea for Malone's perfect ending flashed across his mind. Phillip almost laughed, his impulsive decision to take a shot at the fed forgotten.

His plan would take a little time to set up, but once executed, the revenge would be all the sweeter.

As he drove back into town, he saw the flashing lights of the sheriff's car as it sped past him. No, they'd never catch him. In fact, they'd never have a clue who they were looking for. Just thinking about it made him laugh, and he continued to laugh for a good, long time.

****

Wade slipped into the dark, aware the gunman could still be out there, waiting. Heart racing and adrenaline surging through his body, he jumped over the side railing to the ground. His back to the house, he squatted next to the tall wooden porch, using it as quasi cover. Blood pounded in his ears; his palms sweated.

He tried his best to stay in analytical mode, but kept debating who would be shooting at them? Had he been the target? Or Miranda? It was unlikely she had ticked off someone so badly they'd want her dead, and he had no doubt the bullet wasn't meant as a warning. The shooter had intended for one of them to die, possibly both. He was still angry with her, but he didn't want her dead.

His eyes adjusted to the darkness as he became attuned to every sound around him. Machinery backing up and workers voices from the crash site, the clank of silverware from the Red Cross tent, the lack of nocturnal creatures sounds. A twig snapped off in the distance. But from which direction? It was hard to tell.

He scanned the tree line, looking for any signs of movement or a shadow that didn't belong. Anything to give the location of the shooter. Nothing. Making sure no one lurked around the corner of the house, he stayed low and crept into the trees. Was he walking into a trap? Had the shooting simply been an enticement to get him outside, to get him exactly where he was now in order to kill him? But he'd just gotten to Rock Ledge that morning. Who would be shooting at him? That, he mused, was the question.

Other questions ate at him as he crouched behind a large tree. Was this the time his luck would run out? Like it had for Eric? He hadn't wanted to run into Miranda again, but now that he had, he didn't want to die before he had some answers.

His ability to blend into the foliage had been honed in the jungles and he used it now. Still, there was no sign of the shooter. Frustrated he wasn't finding anyone, he returned to the back porch. The cat leaped out of the darkness, landing on the lower step. Wade had to catch himself from jerking in surprise, or from shooting the animal. The gray cat had seamlessly blended in with the shadows. Keeping his weapon in hand, he patted the animal's head.

"Thanks for the warning, boy." If the cat hadn't jumped when he had earlier, the bullet would have hit either Miranda or himself. Mentally reprimanding himself for not being more aware of his surroundings, he placed a call to his office, informing them of the shooting. A team needed to investigate. That's what he liked about the bureau, you always had backup.

He made his way across the porch, the broken glass crunching underfoot, then knocked.

A moment later Miranda responded. "Wade?"

Good. She'd asked and not automatically opened up, potentially exposing herself to more danger. "Yes, it's me." Before she had the door open more than a crack, the cat zipped through Wade's legs and across the room to his food bowl. Animals.

Once inside, Wade flipped on the lights, glad the curtains were already drawn, and gave himself a minute for his eyes to adjust. He took in the kitchen that looked as if it had been renovated with pristine white cabinets and gray and white granite countertops which complimented the stainless-steel appliances. Then he focused on Miranda. Visibly shaking and her face ghostly pale, she now stood behind the kitchen table with her arms wrapped tightly around herself.

"Are you sure you aren't hurt?"

"I—I don't think so." She looked down at her torso, then backed up before shaking her head.

There was no sign of blood, thank goodness. If anything had happened to her... He *really* didn't want to address that issue at the moment, either physically or mentally. She wasn't acting as if she were hurt, just scared.

"Di—did you find anything? Why did someone shoot at us?"

"Whoever was out there is gone." At least he hoped so. Holstering his weapon, he ran his hands over his face. He should have shaved before leaving the motel. "As to why we were shot at, I don't know. Yet," he added at her stricken look.

She paced the kitchen a bit before she stopped in the center of the room and looked around. "I need to be doing something. Anything." She went to a storage cabinet and pulled out a broom and dustpan, then headed toward the door.

"What do you think you're doing?"

Not looking at him, she said, "Cleaning up the glass. Sebastian might cut himself."

His outstretched arm stopped her. "Not tonight, you aren't. We still need to process the area."

Her face blanched as she took a step away from him. "Oh. Of course. I wasn't thinking."

Wade felt for her. What must she be feeling right now? Terror? Confusion? It wasn't everyday someone tried to kill you. "Besides, it's tempered glass. The cat's paws won't be cut."

Avoiding his gaze, Miranda ducked her head and returned the implements to the closet. Before he had time to say or do anything else, he heard sirens out front. A few minutes later, a loud knock came at the front of the house. The locals. Pushing past her, he let the deputy in. Miranda rushed to the man, hugging him. A prick of *something* struck Wade at the sight. He wasn't sure what the feelings were, but tamped down the sensation.

"Oh, Clay. I'm so glad to see you!" Miranda stepped back, releasing the man in uniform.

"Are you all right?" the deputy asked.

"Yes. Thanks to Wa—um, Agent Malone. Apparently, someone shot at us."

Wade stepped forward and extended his hand. He would've thought they'd have met earlier in the day, but both of them had been busy, though Wade had seen him from a distance. "Special Agent Wade Malone."

"Clay Larson." The man was all business, despite Miranda's obvious affection for him.

Another knock sounded. Larson checked the window, then let Sheriff Bennett inside. Wade succinctly told them everything that had happened as the deputy took notes.

"Let's see the scene. Which way?" the sheriff finally asked.

Wade pointed them toward the kitchen and Miranda started to follow. "Not you," he said flatly. She stiffened. Her eyes narrowed and she set her lips as if she were going to challenge him. He did his best to not bark orders, to keep his tone more neutral, before speaking. "It isn't safe. You need to stay inside."

After a long moment, she finally blew out a heavy breath and nodded. "Can I stay close to the door? To listen?" she asked, a tremor in her voice. She might be acting strong, but she was more affected by the shooting than she let on.

Wade didn't want to admit it out loud, but his

adrenaline levels were nowhere near a normal level, either. It didn't matter how many times he'd been through similar situations, it always affected him. "Just stay away from the window."

As soon as he was outside, she threw the deadbolt. Then they inspected the bullet's impact point and the porch. He pulled out his phone and snapped a couple of pictures. "Looks like the bullet should be in good shape so we can determine the caliber of weapon."

"With luck, prints can be lifted," Bennett added.

Larson took a high-powered light and moved into the trees, looking for traces of the shooter. He concentrated on an area where the shooter might have stood.

Sheriff Bennett raked his hand through his hair. "Any clue why someone might be shooting at you or Ms. Johnson, Agent?"

"I can't speak for her, but a lot of people want to see me dead. Although, I don't know anyone here." *Except Miranda.* "But how did they find out I was here, and how did they get past all the security?"

Bennett paced to the edge of the porch, staring off into the distance. "I can't speculate on the first, but no plan is infallible. Most of the security is around the crash site itself and on the road leading off the highway, not the house. I suppose if someone knew their way around, they could come in through the woods."

"So, a local." Or someone who used to be.

"Most likely. I'm new in town, so I'll ask Larson if he knows of anyone who might want to use you for target practice."

Why now, though? Why here? Did the plane crash have anything to do with someone shooting at him? Or worse, Miranda? A shudder threatened to rack his body, but he suppressed it. The thought of seeing her covered in blood, lying lifeless, sent a hot poker of terror through him. For years he had loved her with all his heart, and now he hated her with just as much fervor. But he didn't want her dead. Especially because of him, because he knew there was no way she had upset someone enough to take pot shots at her.

Frustrated, he resisted the urge to rub a hand over his face. Down to the core of his being, he knew that if the people who had held him captive ever found him, they'd kill him in the most unpleasant of ways. He was well aware of most of those ways because he'd witnessed his captors use the techniques on his fellow captives, and some of the less lethal ones on him. The others hadn't survived the endless torturing. He had not only survived but escaped, much to the captor's displeasure.

Even as an FBI agent, he had people willing to track him down and kill him. One of the reasons why he never developed a serious relationship with anyone.

"This day has been full of unpleasant surprises." Bennett got a faraway look on his face. Recalling the mornings events? Probably. Then the sheriff turned away, walked down the steps and into the woods, looking for his deputy.

A few minutes later, rustling from the trees caught his attention and the other men returned to the house. "Any luck?"

Larson gave a bit of a grin, then held out his phone and showed a picture of where someone had stood and trampled the budding grass. "He was careless and left a little evidence behind. I took pictures of the footprints and direction he headed, but I lost them in the dark. However, I found and bagged fabric fibers clinging to the bark on the tree."

Wade was impressed with the young deputy. "Good job. Most wouldn't have noticed the threads."

He gave a small shrug.

The sheriff looked pleased with the man's performance. "Clay, get some pictures of the damaged door, then dig out the bullet. See if we can get prints off it. With any luck, our guy will be in the system." Bennett turned to Wade. "I'm not sure there's much else we can do tonight, Agent Malone. We're running on a small staff and don't have many resources we can offer you. What's your next move?"

Good question. What was he going to do now? More importantly, what was he going to do with Miranda? "Think you can get Ms. Johnson to stay with someone else tonight so she isn't alone?"

Larson glanced over his shoulder and snorted before he went back to digging the bullet out of the solid wood door. What was that about, Wade wondered?

"She's good friends with Melody Rose. Maybe she'll go there. I can ask," Bennett said.

Wade looked toward the deputy, but this time he remained focused on his task. "If Ms. Johnson won't see reason and leave, I'll stay here and make sure she's safe tonight. By morning, we should be able to have a clearer picture of what happened."

Bennett gave a short nod. Larson finished digging out and bagging the evidence, then he headed to his car. The deputy was young, but appeared competent. The sheriff wouldn't be sticking around long, either. Now all Wade had to do was get Miranda to leave. If she refused, then he had to convince her his spending the night in her home was the best plan of action.

Right after he convinced his heart.

Chapter Four

Randi paced the kitchen floor. What was taking so long, and what had they found? Sorely tempted to go out and help, she reluctantly decided against it. She'd watched enough TV crime shows, plus had enough good sense, to know that wasn't a good idea. The waiting ate at her every nerve ending, though.

Glancing down, she realized her hands were shaking...almost as much as her insides. The evening wasn't cool, but she felt cold all the way to her bones. Never in her life had she experienced anything like this. And never wanted to, again. Did Wade deal with being shot at on a regular basis? How did he handle it? Was he ever afraid? He hadn't acted as if he were, but outward appearances were often deceptive.

Randi wanted to curl into a ball and wish the last hour away. She had been perfectly content to sit on her back porch and block out the workers at the crash site. Then her world had turned upside down—exploding in more ways than one.

Finally, murmured voices drifted in from outside, followed shortly by scraping against the wood. What in the world were they doing?

She was about to throw open the door to find out when Wade knocked, then called out to her. He came inside, followed by the sheriff. Relief that they were all right washed over her a moment before she realized Clay wasn't with them. She peeked outside, hoping to see him. Nothing. Her heart thumped against her chest. Surely, he was okay. Otherwise, the sheriff wouldn't appear so calm. Right?

She frowned. She'd feel better being in the presence of someone she knew and trusted. She'd only met the sheriff that morning, and Wade could no longer be classified as someone she knew. Too many years had passed with too much baggage between them.

The look on Sheriff Bennett's face was as serious as it had been early that morning when he'd brought Melody to the house after she'd been abducted. That look didn't calm her shattered nerves.

"Ms. Johnson. You appear unharmed," the sheriff stated

"I'm not hurt." Thanks to Wade. Would the young man she'd known have reacted the same way? She didn't think so, and was grateful for the man he was now. Another chill ran up her arms. "Did you find anything…or anyone?"

Mute, Wade moved to the side, letting the sheriff take the lead. How could Wade be so calm and collected? How could either of them? Maybe they were used to this sort of thing, but her insides were shaking so hard she felt as if she might throw up. It had taken a bit for the realization to sink in of how much danger she had been in. Here. In her own home. The thought boggled her mind. Hands clasped in front of her, she looked everywhere but at Wade.

Sheriff Bennett broke into her thoughts. "We didn't find the shooter, but did retrieve the bullet. Deputy Larson will send it to the crime lab for analysis."

"Oh, so that's where he is." Did her nerves show? Probably. These were two very intimidating men and Clay being there would have helped put her fears to rest. "I guess he has a lot to do and not babysit me." She tried to laugh, but it came out more of a croak.

Wade's brows had formed into a deep V. Was he frowning at her? Why? Even though the sheriff's expression didn't change, she wanted to clarify. "Clay and I hang out together sometimes."

"Ah, I see." He paused, glanced at Wade, then continued. "And you're right, he's busy. But it isn't safe for you to stay here alone. Perhaps you should go into town and stay with Mrs. Rose tonight. I'd be glad to take—"

She was shaking her head before he even finished his sentence. "Not happening. I refuse to be run out of my own home." She had run when she'd found herself pregnant. Partly because her folks didn't want to be disgraced due to their daughter being an unwed mother, and partly to get away from the unhappy realization that Wade didn't want her, either. She had planted her feet here and she wasn't leaving. She had a gun and was a proficient marksman.

"Ms. Johnson, don't be unreasonable."

She continued shaking her head.

"Fine. If that's the way you want it." Sheriff Bennet walked to the kitchen door, gave her a curt nod, then left.

Wow. That was easy. One down. One to go. "Your turn, Agent Malone. Good night." She wasn't willing to call him by his first name.

He scowled at her, then closed and locked the door. "I'm not leaving."

53

"What did you say?" Surely, he was joking. "There is no need for you to stay. I won't be going outside again so I'll be okay."

"Will you?"

His cold, flat response gave her pause. Or was she in more danger with him here? Her heart stuttered. From being this close to him again? Or fear *of* him? Either way wasn't good.

"Please leave." Randi was proud of the fact her voice didn't wobble. She truly didn't know how to act around him, or what to say to him.

The man stood there as if he were a robot, cold and unfeeling. Yet his eyes reflected something else. For the briefest of moments, she saw the young man she had fallen in love with. It was there and gone in a flash, but she saw it none-the-less.

After several excruciatingly long moments of silence where Randi could have sworn he was looking into her soul, Wade lowered his gaze, then gave his head a slight shake before he went to the window.

"What are you doing?"

"Securing your house." Pausing, he clenched his jaw as he averted his gaze. With a quiet growl, he pushed past her and into the living room. He checked each window. Apparently satisfied, he proceeded to head down the hallway.

She took hold of his arm to stop him, then immediately let go. Even that small amount of contact sent a jolt through her. "There is no need to check each room. As you've already seen, the house is locked up." She did *not* want this man prowling around.

He turned to face her. "Listen, I don't want to be here anymore than you want me here—"

"So leave!"

"—but it's my job to make sure you're safe. I can't do that if I don't check every room." He narrowed his eyes and twisted his head to one side as if trying to work out a puzzle in his mind. "Is there some reason you don't want me to?"

There were so many things she didn't want him to know. Like how she struggled to figure out who she was after he'd left, then learn how to stand on her own two feet and make a living by herself. To realize her own self-worth.

To learn she wanted a true family of her own.

But more importantly, she didn't want him to know about the baby—his baby—she'd given away.

"You mean other than it being invaded by someone who shouldn't be here?" she accused. Pain flashed across his face an instant before it was gone, replaced by his mask of indifference. She shouldn't have said that because she wasn't sure it was true. At the moment, she wasn't sure of anything. There was no way to take it back, though so she simply lifted her chin in defiance.

He stared her down. She stared right back, not wanting to give an inch. Rationally, though, she knew it was in her best interest so relented and stepped aside. "Go on, then," she said through gritted teeth.

His rock-hard facial features didn't change as he moved around her and opened the first door. The once large bedroom was half the previous size and was now her home office. It contained a mid-size desk, an office chair, a cozy bed for Sebastian, and three filing cabinets. Shelves for supplies lined the closet. She'd taken the other half of the room, closed it off, connected it to the next room and created a luxurious master bath for herself. Until Granny's death, they'd shared the one down the hall, but she had always wanted a bathroom all her own. One no one else saw or used.

Ignoring her huff of irritation, he efficiently checked the window in the room and found it locked. She could have told him...not that he'd shown any sign of listening. Next was the hall bathroom with a window too small for an adult to get through. Again, locked.

She tensed when he came to the room on the south side of the house. He hesitated, his hand on the knob. It wasn't her bedroom, and she paled at the thought of him eventually going into her private sanctuary. Had she left the baby album out in plain view? She didn't think so, but eagle eyes here might see it anyway. She had to find a way to keep him out of there. Maybe he'd be so distracted by the contents of this room he'd overlook the remaining room in the house. At least she hoped so.

As he stood there, suspicion glinted in his eyes. She pressed her lips into a thin line and glared. He probably thought he had her all figured out, but he was in for a surprise. She tried to act as detached as him, but she was still apprehensive. What would he think? Approve? Be shocked? Or simply not care? She held her breath.

****

Wade kept a close eye on Miranda's body language. Stiff spine, clenched lips, squinting eyes. She didn't want him here, which made him all the more determined to stay. There was too much between them that needed to be resolved, but she wanted him out too badly. Why? He could have trusted her when she said all the windows were locked, but this gave him a reason to familiarize himself with the layout of the house, and any possible entry points by an intruder. Just because they didn't find the shooter didn't mean he wasn't still out there waiting for another opportunity.

She sucked in a deep breath as his hand touched this particular doorknob. Was it her bedroom? A perverse part of him wanted to see where she slept every night, to see what kind of room she had created for herself. He raised one eyebrow, then pushed open the door and flipped on the light.

She blew out a huff that sounded a lot like satisfaction. This definitely wasn't her bedroom.

He took one step inside, then stopped. Paintings covered almost every inch of the room. Hanging on the wall, leaning against it, some framed, some not, a couple of easels, a bench, brushes, jars of paint, some on the bench but most in an open cabinet.

Wade looked at her. She stood in the hallway, arms crossed over her chest, a bit of uncertainty creasing her features. She nibbled her bottom lip, then, as if realizing what she was doing, stopped. He recalled she used to do that in high school when she was unsure of something. Or anxious. Back then she had craved people's approval, especially her parents...not that she ever received anything from them. Not even their love.

"You did all this?"

That snapped her out of her anxious mode and she dropped her arms. "No. Sebastian likes to play with paint." Her voice dripped with sarcasm.

Wade grunted and began making his way around the room, examining each picture, whether finished or not. There was a riot of colors. Each painting unique. One picture was of an older couple holding hands and smiling at each other as they sat in a porch swing, hanging baskets of multi-colored flowers behind them. A sharp stab hit him in the chest. That was how he'd previously envisioned his golden years, being with Miranda; happy.

Not happening.

"I don't do many portraits but this one touched my heart. It's for their upcoming 60th anniversary."

"You did good." From the corner of his eye, he caught her quick smile before she suppressed it. Was she still the self-conscious girl who craved praise anyplace she could get it? He forced his gaze to the next picture on the wall, a fall landscape. She had a talent for bringing out the rich yellows and oranges with a backdrop of green. A stream cut across the landscape. The sun filtered through the leaves creating almost a halo of the whole scene.

He made his way down the wall, then stopped in front of another portrait, only this one was of an older lady and Miranda as they sat in the swing glider he had seen in her yard. She looked happy, content. Loved. Eyebrow raised, he looked at her.

The hard lines around her mouth softened and wistfulness played around her eyes as she gazed at the picture. "That's Granny Woods. She left me this house when she died. I'm not sure where I'd be right now if she hadn't." Suddenly she dipped her head and looked away, as if she'd revealed more than she wanted. She'd be right.

About to ask her more, he turned around and found a totally different type of painting, almost abstract. Something about the structure, the pattern and the colors struck him. Moving closer, he looked in the lower right-hand corner to see the signature.

He whirled to face her. "*You're* Kathy Hix?"

She shrugged and lifted the corner of her lip in a grin.

He couldn't believe the coincidence. And Special Agent Wade Malone of the FBI did *not* believe in coincidences. Yet, that was all this was. Right? "I've got one of your paintings."

That took her by surprise. "Really? Why? I mean, where did you find it?"

"Art gallery in Kansas City, two years ago."

A slight smile creased her lips. "Oh, yes. Nelson's. I think that was around the time I started placing my art with them. They're good people."

Taking a step back, he studied the picture. "The one I bought isn't as abstract as this, but it reminded me of..." He trailed off. Telling her his picture had reminded him of one she'd painted while they were in art class together as teenagers wouldn't do.

An awkward silence passed between them. Well, more awkward than it already was.

Finally, she cleared her throat, then said, "I guess you liked it enough to buy it. I do quite a few abstracts."

"Freestyle."

Her green eyes widened as her hand came up to her throat. "Yes," she whispered. "You—you remembered my pet name for it. The art teacher hated that I refused to call my paintings abstract, but I needed something that was uniquely mine. I've since learned to be more practical, especially when marketing my work."

"Makes sense." Now it was his turn to shrug.

Then he spied the painting on the easel. Shocked,

he couldn't take his eyes off of the horror and destruction depicted on the canvas. Why hadn't that been the first thing he'd seen when he walked into the room? Miranda had obviously "free styled" it, letting what she'd seen early that morning flow out of her.

Wade had been there, had seen everything there was to see at the crash site, and expected to have nightmares about it. But knowing a civilian, Miranda in particular, had seen it and would also have similar nightmares, punched him in the gut.

Arms wrapped around her waist, she stood stiffly, leaning against the doorjamb and not looking at the painting. Her face had paled. His first impulse was to drape a cloth over the painting, and then give her a reassuring hug. Instead, he checked the windows and drew the curtains before he herded her farther into the hallway, doing his best to not touch her. He then closed the door behind him.

There was one more room to check…her bedroom obviously. "Are the windows in your room locked?"

She shot him a look. "Of course. As I said, you're wasting your time."

"And I told you, I need to make sure everything is secure."

"It is. Locked up tight as a drum. I have a shotgun and know how to use it. I figure the sound of the gun being racked would certainly scare anyone away. Plus, I keep a can of wasp spray as a nonlethal deterrent next to my bed. I'm not naïve, and I'm certainly not careless. Nor helpless."

No. She wasn't. "Would you actually shoot someone? Or try to talk them out of the house first?"

"If my life was threatened, you bet I'd shoot.

Hesitate and you're dead."

Smart girl. Wade didn't want to admit it, but his respect for her went up. First, he finds out she's a top-notch artist, then learns she knew how to defend herself. A far cry from the withdrawn girl he'd left behind.

They still needed to have that discussion about their past, but it was late, and every bone in his body ached. Someone out there had shot at them, and whether he was the target or her, it didn't matter. He'd stand watch to make sure nothing happened during the night.

"Go to bed, Miranda."

"And where do you intend to sleep?" She glanced at the closed door to her bedroom, then back at him.

"I don't. If I get fatigued, I'll take a short nap on the couch."

She looked as if she might challenge his statement, then gave her head a small shake. Retrieving a pillow and a light blanket from the hall closet, she took them to the living room and dropped them on the couch. "In case you get too 'fatigued' and need some rest, you'll be more comfortable with these."

Giving him one last searching look, she went back down the hall. A moment later her door closed. He sighed. What was he doing here? With her? Too tired to delve into it deeper, he turned out all the lights except the light over the stove, which served well as a nightlight.

He spent the next couple of hours pacing from one end of the house to the other. That included checking the outside perimeter as well. Eventually, though, exhaustion pulled at him and, after a couple more rounds of checking the house, he sank down on the couch. He'd rest his eyes for a few minutes, then he'd go back to his patrolling. The rhythmic ticking of the wall clock relaxed him. His eyelids drooped as his body slumped on the cushions.

The old recurring nightmare hit him with a vengeance.

Chapter Five

Randi felt Wade's gaze on her back as she walked down the hall. Why was it so long all of a sudden? She squelched the urge to run, not wanting to give him the satisfaction of seeing her squirm. The man came across so intense, a complete opposite of the boy she'd grown up with.

Finally, she stepped into her bedroom and Sebastian brushed past her before she firmly closed the door. Wondering where her well-ordered world had gone, she sat on the side of the bed, and then pulled the white photo album off the nightstand's lower shelf. Keeping the precious memories close comforted her. Flipping to the first page, she smiled at the picture of her daughter the day she'd been born. Randi gently ran her fingers over the image of her little girl, all pink and pretty wearing a bow bigger than her head. Longing stabbed her. If only she'd been able to keep the baby.

She sighed, then reeled in the emotions. Giving up the child for adoption had been the best option for the baby…and the only option for Randi. Life wasn't fair and she'd learned to live with it a long time ago. Her saving grace had been the adopting family had agreed to an open adoption so Randi had kept in touch with them over the years. Katie, her sweet daughter, lived in Fayetteville, only a couple of hours away and her parents were doing an amazing job of raising her. Randi's daughter was in the best possible place and she would do anything to protect the child.

What would Wade do if he found out? Try to rip her away from her parents? Too afraid to ponder that question, Randi flipped through the album, reliving each moment of Katie's life. From first steps, to teething, to kindergarten graduation, to last year's soccer games and all the holidays in between. Randi had gone and watched Katie play soccer whenever possible. She was a talented athlete. Pride for her offspring settled in her chest, making her smile. She loved that child with every ounce of her being.

Laying the book on the dresser an hour later, Randi turned and went into her bathroom and got ready for bed. Not that sleep would come. Not with Wade down the hall. She'd heard him quietly walking the hallway several times, the squeaky floorboard near her office giving him away. It was strange, knowing he was in her home, keeping her safe. Physically, anyway. The danger to her heart was another matter altogether.

By the time she was ready for bed, Sebastian was curled up next to her pillow instead of at the foot of the bed like he normally did. Bless his heart. He knew she needed more comfort tonight. How animals always sensed that was beyond her, but she was grateful. She climbed between the sheets and pulled the cat close, his purr lulling her to sleep.

Randi tossed and turned, her dreams plagued with the horrific images from this morning, alternating with visions of the man from her past who had invaded her home. One mixed with the other until they had almost merged into one confusing nightmare. Daylight and darkness. A longed-for wish come true…to death. She was lost in a world where there was no way out.

Sudden pressure on her stomach jolted her awake, releasing her from her prison. Sebastian licked her face a couple of times, but when she moved to stroke the cat who'd landed on her belly, he abandoned her to go to the door, then jumped back to her side. Before she had time to react, he went to the door again. What in the world? His pitiful wails sounded as if he were going to be sick so she climbed from bed to let him out. Only he didn't run down the hall to the litter box, nor did he throw up as she'd half expected. He stood in the doorway and looked back at her, waiting. Then she heard it. A loud, soul-rendering moan. Wade.

Shaking off the remnants of her own horrible dream, she pulled on her robe and scurried barefoot down the hallway, the cat leading the way. He stopped at the side of the couch and looked up her, almost as if he was asking her to fix Wade. Randi swore the cat was part dog the way he acted sometimes. Wade let out another loud groan. For a brief moment, she wondered if the bullet that had shattered her storm door had hit him and he'd somehow managed to conceal it from her. But when she reached his side, it was obvious he was sound asleep, having a nightmare. No bullet wound. No blood, thank goodness.

She knelt next to the sofa, debating what to do. His moans were loud and he sounded as if he were in terrible pain. He had to be hurting, even if it was only a dream. But how to help him? She'd never been around anyone who had nightmares, but Melody had told her about soldiers with PTSD who had severe nightmares and that you needed to be careful waking them. For one thing, you could get punched. Or worse.

Randi glanced at the gun Wade had left on the coffee table. Any sudden moves on her part, and she had no doubts he'd be able to reach and draw the weapon faster than she'd be able to react. The thought almost drove her back to her bedroom. Before she could rise, he let out a heart-wrenching groan. She had to do something…anything, so she did the first thing that came to mind and began talking to him in a soothing voice.

Initially, he didn't respond to her and kept thrashing and moaning. The thought of what had happened to him to cause a nightmare like this tore at her. For some reason, she didn't think it was from today's crash. Her heart went out to him and she gently laid her hand on his shoulder.

Touching him again, after all these years, brought back a flood of bittersweet memories. Of him holding her, making her feel as if she were the most cherished person in the world. Of always feeling warm and safe within his arms. Of making tender, sweet love, then later in the night, more passionately as if they couldn't get enough of each other. Of falling asleep in each other's arms, clinging to each other for as long as possible. The next day, he'd left on that flight and never returned. Over the years, she'd relived their one and only night together over and over in her mind. If only they'd had more time. If only he hadn't left…

Gripping his arm tighter, she said, "Wade. It's all right. You're safe. No one is going to hurt you." She took a long breath, her heart swelling, then added, "I've got you. It's okay. I'm here."

As soon as she murmured those last words, he

settled. Almost immediately, his breathing evened out and he was fast asleep again. She sat there, still touching him, still remembering their past. Then, she slowly withdrew. He didn't want her anymore, had no need of her. And if he ever learned about the baby, he'd hate her for the rest of his days. A tear slid down her cheek for all they'd lost, for the life she knew in her soul they'd never have together.

Quietly, she stood, picked up Sebastian, and tip-toed back to her room.

****

Wade couldn't believe he'd spent the night at Miranda's. Granted, they had thought her life was in danger, but what had possessed him to think he could stay there and keep his emotions in check? His recurring nightmare from the jungle had come back full force during the night. Miranda's presence had been the only thing that had helped. Her soft cooing and gentle touch surprised him, making him want more. Even the darned cat wanted to help him and had kept touching Wade's hand with his nose.

It had taken everything in him to not let Miranda know her softly spoken words had woken him, and that he was aware of her presence. The one thing he'd learned while a captive was to fake sleep while wide awake. With her so close, it had been harder than he would have thought.

Thankfully, she hadn't stayed by his side too long, and she and the cat had returned to bed. Her light floral fragrance had lingered, though, making it difficult for him to go back to sleep. Although, the thought of revisiting the horrible dream that had plagued him since his return to the States was enough to keep him awake.

He'd listened to every creak, every subtle sound of the older house. The continued work at the crash site served as white noise, but at least there hadn't been anything else alarming around the house. Refusing to stay on the couch, he had made a few more trips inside, avoiding the squeaky board in the hall that gave away his presence.

Just after dawn, satisfied Miranda was safe, he'd left without bothering to wake her or tell her goodbye, then stopped at the motel for a change of clothes…and a cold shower. He wasn't sure if he needed the shower to dispel the images of a jungle going up in flames with people trying to kill him, or of her scent that permeated every inch of her home. And now him. At any rate, he was determined to concentrate on why he was here in the first place…his friend's dead face flashed across his mind.

He shook off the image as he pulled into the parking lot of the Tangled Rose Café and found a spot on the far side. A small bell above the door announced his presence when he entered the establishment. The place lived up to its name. A huge wild rose bush had been painted on the back wall. The artist had even included the thorns. Had Miranda painted the mural? Possibly. Probably. Had she signed it? He resisted the urge to go look.

Vinyl records, pictures of movie stars from previous eras, and various football logos took up space on a side wall. A long counter and the kitchen were off to the right. Freshly brewed coffee, along with the sizzle of frying bacon, made his mouth water.

"Welcome to The Tangled Rose." A very pregnant waitress sat on a stool at the register and handed him a menu. "Take a seat anywhere you can find one. Someone will be with you shortly, but please be patient. We're a bit overwhelmed right now."

He could see why. Only one other waitress was working, the woman who'd served them sandwiches at Miranda's the day before, and she was moving at a whirlwind pace.

Several people turned to stare at him. His jacket, embossed with the FBI logo, stuck out like a sore thumb. Normally, such scrutiny didn't bother him, but this morning he was still disoriented from the prior evening, and he found the unwanted attention unsettling. To make up for it, he scowled, resulting in most everyone averting their gazes. Good.

Wade nodded to the sheriff, who sat at the crowded counter, then found an empty table in the middle of the room. Seeing Bennett was a stark reminder Wade had neglected his job, again, by not checking the woods for more clues as to the shooter before leaving Miranda's this morning. Being around her was a major distraction. One he couldn't afford.

He resisted the urge to growl at himself for being so careless. Instead, he concentrated on the menu. Not surprising, it contained what he'd found in hundreds of other diners and cafes across the country. Sooner than he expected, the waitress appeared at his table.

"Morning, agent. What can I get you?"

"Melody, isn't it?"

"Yes, it's nice of you to remember."

"It was kind of you to feed everyone yesterday. It sure was appreciated." Wade gave her a brief smile.

"No big deal. Glad Randi and I could help. Now what would you like to eat?"

He felt bad for making small talk when she was obviously so busy and wondered why Miranda wasn't helping her out. Then again, maybe she wasn't much of a waitress. Who knew? "Coffee and the number one."

"You got it. It'll be right out." She hurried away, returning a short time later with his coffee, before waiting on another table.

The small building was packed with customers. From the looks of them, the vast majority were reporters, but some were locals. Of course, some could be people who simply got a thrill out of someone else's misfortune, like the scavengers who'd gotten there before the National Guard had arrived, cleared everyone out, and then cordoned off the area.

So how had someone gotten close enough to Miranda's house to shoot at them? That question continued to nag at him. Perhaps a local who had come in through the woods. Was there a back road or even a path someone could take? How far around the National Guard perimeter would they have to go to get to the house? He pulled out his notebook and made a notation, adding it to the list of things to check. He wanted to find out before he left.

He glanced up at the sheriff, who was casing the room while he ate, the same as Wade was doing. From the dark circles under Bennett's eyes, he hadn't gotten much sleep. No one did during one of these situations. *Except I managed to sleep long enough to have that nightmare.*

Wade had just taken another sip of coffee when the hairs on the back of his neck stood up, the same as they'd done at the crash site yesterday. Moving his head as little as possible, he scanned the room. With the look of a tiger ready to pounce, a female reporter watched him closely. Wade wanted to tell her she was wasting her energy if she thought she'd actually get an interview with him. He had to give her credit for not barging over to his table, though. Perhaps his dark scowl kept her at bay. He wasn't in the mood to deal with the press.

His spine kept tingling. No, the reporter wasn't the reason for his unease. Several of the locals kept glancing his way, and he dismissed all of them. Except for a man at a back table. He might appear to be local, but Wade would bet otherwise. There was something about him that gave Wade pause. Over the years, he'd come to recognize a person who had spent time behind bars...or who needed to *be* behind bars. Despite the fact the man kept looking down at his food, every time Wade looked his direction, he'd been staring at Wade with cold, dead eyes.

Wade made a mental note to ask the sheriff if he knew him. Although, since Bennett had only been in town a few weeks, probably not. Still, Wade kept an eye on him. A quick glance at the sheriff confirmed his instinct. From the scowl on Sheriff Bennett's face, he didn't like the looks of the man, either. But, until he did something illegal, there was no reason to question or detain him. Wade had never seen him before, but there was something about the unsavory character that seemed familiar. If only he could pinpoint what that was.

His food arrived, and his thoughts went back to the crash site. Would they get most of the debris retrieved today? Would they find any other body parts?

Would Miranda let him back in her house?

****

Miranda had heard Wade moving around early the next morning, but, like a coward, she had stayed hidden. Once he'd left, she finally emerged from her room.

He might have slept peacefully the rest of the night after his nightmare, but she hadn't. She'd run *what-ifs* through her mind all night long. Should she have awakened him? Or simply have left him alone? What was the dream about? The horrific plane crash? Or something else? Too chicken to ask or to confront him, she had done what she'd always done and made herself invisible, not willing to stick her neck out for more rejection.

She'd learned her lesson well as a child and found it difficult to completely overcome as an adult. Her stepfather had made sure she knew she was worthless, and her mother had gone along with it. The longer the two were married, the more like him her mom had become. Now, there was little of the woman left whom Randi had loved as a little girl. They'd been a warm and loving family before her real dad left. Then Ray moved in and everything changed practically overnight. They had done an exemplary job of cutting Randi out of their lives after she'd gotten pregnant. Fine. She was better off without them. Neither of them was worth her time or energy, and definitely weren't worth her love.

Now, she stood with a steaming cup of coffee in her hands, wondering where Wade was, what he was doing. Did he go directly back to the crash site, or to his motel? Had the sheriff found who had shot at them? *Why?* she wanted to know. Running all the possibilities through her mind gave her a headache.

A peek out front told her just as many people were on her property as there had been yesterday, maybe more if she counted the Red Cross who were set up on the far side of her large yard. She was almost afraid to even step outside to drink her morning coffee on the back porch like she normally did. A quick glance reminded her of the shattered storm door that needed to be cleaned up. It could wait. Instead, she took a seat at the kitchen table and stared into the cup she had cradled in her hands. Sebastian curled around her legs, rubbing his head against her and purring.

"Thanks for always being there for me, sweetie." She reached down and scratched behind his ear, appreciating his presence more than ever. She might have rescued the cat, but Randi felt as if he had saved her. Until she'd gotten him, she hadn't realized how lonely she'd become since Granny's death.

Finally, she stood and set her empty coffee cup in the sink, then took a deep breath. "You know, I don't intend to become a prisoner in my own home. I don't need to actually be here for the men to replace the storm door, so think I'll go for a ride. It'll be nice to clear my head. What do you think?" She looked down at the cat, who was content to preen himself. Huh, well, as long as his food bowl was full and he had water, the cat was happy.

Laughing, she headed to the bedroom to change into her jeans, boots, leather jacket and helmet. Now if the ruts in her road weren't too deep, maybe she wouldn't get dumped off the motorcycle before she got to the highway.

Thirty minutes later she pulled the Harley into the gas station in Rock Ledge. Ignoring the stares, or admiring looks, by a few people, she killed the engine and climbed off. She wasn't sure where she was going, but it always paid to have a full tank of gas beforehand. Maybe down to Nail and around. She'd play it by ear.

"Nice ride."

Startled, she glanced over at the man speaking to her.

"Um, thanks." She wasn't in the mood to talk, especially to strangers, and especially not after last night.

"I admire a woman who isn't afraid to tackle a large machine. Kudos." He nodded and smiled as he turned back to pumping his gas.

Randi relaxed. It still amazed her the number of people who had a hard time visualizing a woman riding a Hog. A few years ago, there hadn't been that many, but the numbers had grown.

"You got Screaming Eagles on there, I see." With his arms crossed, the man now leaned against his car as he studied the bike.

"Um, yes." She noticed the tattoos on his hands and arms. Lots of people had them now days, but his looked different. Not sure why they were different, just that they were.

He shook his head and focused on her. "Sorry. My brother and I used to ride dirt bikes as kids. Haven't been on a two-wheeler in a long time. I miss it. Seeing you on one inspires me."

"Thanks. You should get back out there. You'd enjoy it, especially on the winding roads around here."

"I might do that." His pumped clicked off, and a minute later he pulled out of the station.

Randi turned her attention back to her own fueling,

making sure she didn't overfill. Once she pocketed the receipt, she pulled her gloves back on, snapped her face shield in place, then climbed on the Softtail. She glanced toward the café down the street. Was Wade standing there watching? Waiting a moment to see if he'd acknowledge that he'd seen her turned out to be a fruitless endeavor. He didn't move. Okay, then.

The bike roared to life, drowning out every other sound and thought from her mind as the deep rumble soothed her soul. All she needed was some wind on her face shield. Making a snap decision on the direction of her ride, she pulled onto the road and headed for the highway leading south. Right now, she needed a really winding road to get her head straight. So what if it took several hours to complete the ride? At least she wouldn't be near the crash site.

****

Getting breakfast had taken longer than Wade had anticipated. He had just reached his car when the sound of a motorcycle caught his attention. He watched as the biker stopped at the gas station down the block from the café. The rider flipped the face shield up, and he realized it was a woman. Was that Miranda? He stared as she got off the big machine.

A car pulled into the lot, drawing his attention. Deputy Clay Larson exited the vehicle. "Excuse me, deputy," Wade called.

The young man stopped. "Agent Malone."

He nodded toward the gas station. "Is that Miranda Johnson on a motorcycle?"

Larson laughed. "Yeah. Ain't that something? She went with me and Roy Maddox, the café's cook, to a rally in Fayetteville a few years ago, and got hooked.

Decided she didn't like riding behind either one of us, so got her own bike. She's a natural."

Wade's stomach roiled, not sure of what he felt at the thought of her clinging to someone else. Of wrapping her arms around another man, or pressing her breasts against his back. Jealousy? Envy? But after all these years, he had no claim on her, didn't *want* any claim on her, so he tamped down the unwanted feelings. "So you're dating?" He did his best to keep the accusing tone out of his voice, not sure if he succeeded.

Larson gave him a sidewise glance, but didn't react otherwise. "No. We're just friends. Randi doesn't date much. Don't know why 'cause she's a lot of fun to be around. Hangs out with us at the pizza parlor sometimes and shoots pool, or goes for rides with us. She handles the bike well and is a cautious rider, which is a good thing. A lot can happen on these roads."

"Yes, I imagine it can. Thanks, deputy. I'll let you get to your breakfast." He had been talking to Larson, but he'd kept his gaze on Miranda.

"Anytime." He walked away, not bothering to pay any more attention to what was happening at the gas station.

The leery looking man from the café was talking to Miranda. From this vantage point, they looked pretty chummy. Before long, the guy left. A few moments later, she climbed on her bike, glanced toward Wade, then headed in the same direction as the other man. Larson was right, she was a natural. A small smile played at the corner of his lips, proud she handled the huge machine so well. He had no right to feel this way, but this woman was a world apart from the shy girl she'd been in high school. Her compassion from the prior evening during his nightmare clung to him, soothed him.

Wade frowned. Why had she been talking to the unsavory character? Was he connected to the fugitive on board the plane? Did he have anything to do with the plane going down? And that it went down on her property? Coincidences? Wade didn't believe in them as a general rule. This case was riddled with them, though. His mind crafted all sorts of scenarios, none of them good. Distrust of almost everyone while investigating a case was his normal mode of operation. So, where were they going?

Needing to know, he headed for his car when his phone rang. The home office. He had no choice but to take the call. Two additional agents were being dispatched to investigate the shooting and he had to meet them within the hour. One last glance at the road Miranda had gone down, and he discarded his plans. The other agents were a reminder of the shooting from last night and of how dangerous his job was on a regular basis. Time to move back into work mode and forget about the woman whose presence had kept him awake most of the night.

****

Wade shouldn't have been surprised to see Agents Paul Smith and Larry Wesson step off the plane. Besides himself, they were the best at investigative work. Totally opposite in appearance, one short and stocky, the other tall and thin, the two complimented each other in every other way. They even seemed to read each other's minds, which is one of the reasons the two worked so well together.

Their first stop was the sheriff's office to collect the evidence from the locals. Bennett was more than happy to turn everything over to them. Wade felt the same way. Letting the other agents take charge was a relief, though he would never let on to them. Miranda had become a distraction for him and that distraction could cost him his life.

Next stop, the scene of the crime...Miranda's house.

For the next few hours, the men meticulously went over the entire area where the shooting had taken place. But Wade kept losing his focus by simply being near the back porch where he had covered her body with his. The feel of her beneath him brought back memories that should still be under lock and key. But weren't. Not anymore. More than once, one of the other men had to call his name a second time to get his attention. Grinding his back teeth, he forced himself to concentrate.

They followed the trail of the shooter into the forest, but eventually lost it. Too bad they didn't have a K-9 to follow the scent. Though, the shooter most likely had a vehicle parked close by, so the dog would've lost the scent at that point. Frustration ate at him as he kept running scenarios through his mind as to why they'd been shot at and who was behind it.

Mostly, though, he wanted to know where Miranda was right now.

****

Randi loved the feel and rumble of the motorcycle under her and opened the throttle, appreciating the view of the wonderful Ozark Mountains. Spring had arrived, and she planned to enjoy every minute of the day. The elm and redbud trees had started leafing out, crocus had pushed their way through and were budding, and the grass had started to turn green. The air felt clean and fresh and she welcomed the coming season.

She took her time, making a stop or two along the way. Over three hours later, she pulled down her drive, slowing to almost a crawl in order to keep the Harley in an upright position on the rough road. After the cleanup was done, her first order of business would be to get her road rebuilt and back into the shape it had been before.

Every muscle in her body ached. This was the first time she'd been out this spring, and she'd forgotten how tiring it was to maintain control of the large bike. She was more out of shape than she thought. Not only was she tired, but she needed to pee something fierce.

Reaching the house without dumping the bike was a minor miracle, in her opinion. But she'd done it, both going and coming. She parked in the detached garage and turned around, intending to head to the house. And the bathroom. Except Wade stood there, looking all stoic and like a piece of granite. Across the yard behind him, she noticed two more men wearing FBI jackets as they looked her direction. Or were they watching Wade? A minute later, they climbed into a car and left.

"Not now." Her full bladder could tell a bathroom was nearby, and if she didn't hurry, there was a very real possibility she was going to embarrass herself.

"We need to talk," he insisted.

Randi ignored his statement and pushed past him, lowering the garage door as she went. Wade made a motion to block her path, but she deftly stepped around him. She stalked away with him not too far behind, but was able to get inside the house and close the door in his face. Now, if she could only make it to the bathroom before she wet herself.

She took her time and, once done, put her riding gear away. A check out the front window confirmed Wade was nowhere in sight. She wasn't sure what his problem was, but he'd looked as if she'd done something wrong. Since when was going for a ride against the law? Men.

Sebastian popped down out of his cat tree and demanded some loving. Always ready to oblige, she curled up in her recliner, spread the afghan across her lap and prepared herself for the almost twenty-pound feline. After he got through kneading his paws, he settled down. Exhaustion tugged at her. With her feet propped up and the weight of the cat on her lap, she drifted off to sleep, Wade's image invading her dreams.

Chapter Six

Randi awoke from her nap with a stiff neck. Sebastian had settled in, anchoring her to the chair. After several gentle nudges, and one not so gentle, she finally got him moving. If only she could get herself up as easily. It took a couple of tries, but she managed to stand. Wow, was she ever sore.

Rubbing her neck while stretching her back, she wandered around the house. But nothing took her mind off the activity happening so close by. *And Wade.* Despite the ride earlier, she felt as if she might suffocate inside her home…last night kept echoing through her mind. What would Wade have done if she'd leaned over and kissed him? Would he have welcomed her kiss, or while in his dream state, picked up his gun and shot her? The prior, she hoped. More than likely, the latter, though. She'd never know, but the wondering kept eating at her. And what had been his problem when she'd gotten home from her ride?

Finally, she couldn't stand it anymore and picked up the phone and called her best friend.

Melody answered on the second ring. "Hey. What's up?"

"Can I come over? I need to get out of here for a while." Her voice sounded strained, even to her own ears.

"Of course. You don't need to ask; you know you're always welcome."

"Thanks. I'll be there in a bit." Randi hoped her heavy sigh hadn't echoed through the phone before she'd disconnected, then dismissed her worries. Mel would be there for her no matter what. Twenty minutes later, she sat in her friend's kitchen.

"I've got everything ready for margaritas. Or would you rather have iced tea? I've got a fresh pitcher in the fridge," Melody said.

The reason why she'd wanted to come over slammed into her and she felt as deflated as a left-over party balloon. "A margarita, please."

"Gotcha. Alcohol it is."

Once they were both seated at the table, with drinks in their hands, Randi couldn't bring herself to open up about the things bothering her—like one gorgeous FBI agent who haunted her dreams. As if Melody understood, and by unspoken agreement, for the next couple of hours they talked about all the strangers in town, the weather changes, a new business going in down the block from the café, and all the minor gossip that made up small towns. Mundane stuff. Randi drained the last of the drink she'd been nursing all this time and stood.

"Hey, wait. You aren't leaving, are you?"

Randi smiled, knowing it didn't quite reach her eyes. "I think I need to get on home. I've taken up enough of your time."

"Don't be silly. You know I've enjoyed this evening. I needed a diversion, too."

They hugged. "Thanks for letting me hang out."

"Was there something specific you wanted to tell

me tonight?"

Randi thought about everything she hadn't told her friend. No. She'd come here to get away from those memories, those gut-wrenching feelings, and it had worked. "Nothing specific, at least not anything I want to bother you with right now. I just needed some company, but it's getting late so I should get going. I know how early you have to get up in the morning."

"Oh, I'll be all right. I think I'm still keyed up from all that's happened the last couple days, too, so doubt I'll fall asleep easily." At the front door, they hugged. "You take care of yourself and be careful. I've seen a couple of people in the café who I wouldn't want to meet in daylight, much less at night. Personally, I'll be glad when all this is over and all those strangers are gone."

Randi hesitated a second as sadness enveloped her...Wade's image floated across her mind. "Yeah. It won't be the same when all of them leave."

They hugged again, then Randi made her way to her car and left. Before she'd gone far, she stopped on a dark side street and let the tears fall that had been stinging her eyes. She cried for the people who had died in the crash, for the man she had lost so long ago, and for the life they'd never have together. It didn't matter that he was still alive. He'd never be hers again.

After her tears were spent, she dried her eyes, blew her nose and pulled back onto the road. She drove slowly, dreading going back to the noise from the crash site. Even with the TV on and the house closed up, she swore she heard every little sound. Life was what it was, though, so no sense in stalling any longer.

Dodging the emergency vehicles still clogging her

driveway, she found another car parked in front of the house. Her heart fluttered a moment before a rock dropped into the pit of her stomach.

Wade.

****

Wade hadn't expected Miranda to be gone…not this late in the day. He still wasn't sure what he wanted from her, but he did know they needed to discuss their past. If he left without finding out why she hadn't waited on him, why she'd disappeared, that piece of unfinished business would haunt him. He hated not having everything tied up into neat packages.

That included the man she met up with earlier in the day. He was definitely a loose end. Did he have anything to do with the prior evening's events? If so, and if she knew, would she tell him? Perhaps he shouldn't be obsessing about the guy, but he couldn't help it. The man was no good. Wade knew it in his gut.

So here he sat, waiting. The sun had set, and the air now held a decided chill. Spring would bring much warmer temperatures, but he'd be long gone before the trees fully leafed-out or the flowers bloomed. He briefly wondered if Miranda planted a lot of flowers. She certainly had room out here, but he only saw a couple of beds close to the house. What else didn't he know about her besides the fact she rode a huge motorcycle and painted? Finding the answer to that wasn't why he was here, but he'd like to know all the same.

Just to satisfy his curiosity.

Just so he wouldn't have any unresolved issues bugging him.

Just to have a complete image of her and her surroundings in his mind once he left.

He sighed and mentally kicked himself. Checking his watch, he realized he'd been here over an hour. He'd stayed longer than he should have. His curiosity still ate at him, though. Where was she?

She might be on a date. The young deputy might not think she went out much, but even in small towns, people managed to keep parts of their lives private. Wade wasn't interested in her, would never be interested in her again. He simply needed closure so he could lock up that one unresolved piece of his life before he moved forward without ever looking back.

Liar.

He reached for the ignition key when headlights from an oncoming vehicle bounced down the lane. It could be one of the rescue workers or the sheriff, but he doubted it. Sure enough, her burnt orange SUV pulled into the drive and parked next to him. Initially, she stayed in the car, so he waited.

Miranda finally got out and headed toward the house without looking in his direction. He followed, giving her space, but remained close enough she wouldn't be able to get inside the house and close the door in his face. Been there, done that, he thought ruefully.

The dark drapes in the house were closed, and the porch light was on. Good. She wasn't taking chances. Except for coming home after dark all alone. Did she have a weapon on her? Probably not. He should tell her to carry some Mace. Small. Easy to use. Or, heck, even that can of wasp spray she said she kept by her bed.

But who worried about needing protection at your own home, especially out in the country? Not many people did, but should…last night a vivid testament to that fact.

She unlocked the door, then turned toward him, the porch light casting a pallor to her skin. Her eyes were puffy. Had she been crying?

"Agent Malone." Her voice wobbled. "I wondered when you'd show up."

"There are a few things we need to go over before I leave town."

Her chin trembled as she raised it. Straightening her back, she met his gaze head-on. "Strange. I would've thought you'd have said whatever you wanted to say last night. Or this morning before you left. Since you took off without a word, I assumed there was nothing left to discuss."

She was right, and he almost felt a twinge of guilt for sneaking out like he had. Almost. But now he needed to get inside and from her sharp look of defiance, he had to be a little contrite.

"I apologize for leaving like I did. I appreciate the use of your couch." Wade tried to sound sincere. Truly he did, but from her expression he'd missed the mark. Badly. If he didn't say something else, she'd leave him standing here facing a closed door. Again.

She surprised him when she blew out a hard breath and said, "Fine. Come in." Dropping her keys into a bowl inside the door and her jacket on the nearby coat rack, she left him to follow.

She stopped in the living room of the small but efficient house and turned to face him. His gaze swept the now familiar room. Except for the renovated kitchen, not much else appeared different than it probably had a decade or two ago. Twelve-inch planks of grooved, pecan colored paneling lined the two inside living room walls. Cream colored outer walls, two windows, one large with the cloth sofa in front of it, the other smaller and by the front door. Both covered with heavy, dark green drapes. A worn leather recliner faced a flat screen TV on a coffee table. A small table sat next to the recliner with a paperback book on it, and a few landscape pictures dotted the walls. Homey. Warm. Inviting. All adjectives that described her house.

Wade was pretty sure the last adjective wouldn't be applied to him shortly. "What were you doing with that man this morning?"

Her brows formed into a deep V and, for a moment, she looked genuinely confused. Then she swung around and plopped into the recliner. Buying time to think of a comeback? He'd seen every trick in the book.

"What are you talking about?" She looked at him as if he'd lost his mind. "What man?"

"The one in the dark blue car." Wade had seen the prison tats on the guy when he'd left the café. Was she involved with him somehow? He wouldn't have thought it of her but, he reminded himself a person changed a lot in nine years. Look at him. He moved close to her chair, braced his feet apart and glared down at her in an effort to intimidate her. She'd done nothing to warrant these tactics from him, but some perverse part of him wanted to prove she had gleefully walked away from his love all those years ago.

She craned her neck to look up at him, her eyebrows raised, then said flatly, "I should've left you outside. Where you belong."

Wade narrowed his eyes. He wasn't sure what to expect from her, but pushback wasn't it. Before he could respond, Sebastian padded into the room, took one look at him towering over her, and hissed at him. Actually hissed. Just the night before, the cat had been affectionate. Apparently, it sensed Wade's hostility and didn't like it. Not one little bit. Instead of jumping up in her lap, the cat sat in front of her as if he were guarding her. And damned if Wade didn't find that admirable. And funny.

And he wasn't dumb enough to challenge the animal.

Wade moved to the far end of the couch and sat on the edge of the seat. He wanted as much space between him and Sebastian as possible in case the cat decided to defend his owner. Wade had seen his claws and didn't relish the thought of coming into contact with them. "Look. Let me start over. I saw you with a guy at the gas station, then you followed him. What business do you have with him?"

She blinked, leaned forward, and picked up the cat, whose ears were still laid back. It also didn't lie down. Instead, it sat up, watching Wade intently. "I have no idea who... Wait. There was some guy who admired my bike while I was getting gas, but I don't know him. Had never seen him before."

Wade noticed the cat still wasn't purring and was watching him closely. He found it harder to focus on her with the cat acting as her guardian than he would've thought. Finally, he tore his gaze away from the animal and refocused on her. "Then why did you follow him?" he accused. She could have gone three different directions from the corner station, but she'd followed him.

She looked at him so long he thought she wouldn't

answer. Finally, she said, "You have gone off the deep end, Malone. I have no idea who that man is and don't care. I didn't pay any attention to which direction he went. He could have gone to the moon for all I know. I was just out enjoying a ride." Her tone changed to an accusatory one at the end.

He studied her long moments. Was she telling the truth? "So, you're saying the man at the gas station, who just happened to go the same direction as you, was a fluke?"

"Duh." At least she wasn't glaring at him anymore. "For the record, I didn't see him anywhere along the way, and might not have recognized him if I did. You know, to be with the FBI, you don't seem to have a lot on the ball. Maybe you should work on that."

Blowing out a deep breath, he sat back and shook his head. Being around her made him lose the sharp edge he normally had during a case. Though he still wanted to know more about the man. The guy was trouble and, eventually, Wade would have to deal with him.

"Listen, I saw him in the café earlier. I'd be careful around him if I were you."

Frowning, she asked, "Any reason?" She stroked the cat, who had finally settled back against her and begun to purr.

"No. Nothing specific. Just a feeling." He didn't add those feelings were seldom wrong. He seriously needed to get himself back on track. "I truly am sorry. It's just…"

He sat there staring at a picture on the wall for a long moment. Eventually, he returned his gaze to her. "I don't normally jump to conclusions like this. It's seeing you, and...and I knew one of the marshals on the plane."

Her entire demeanor changed. "Oh, Wade. I'm so sorry. Were you close?"

His throat constricted. He swallowed a couple of times, then nodded, unable to get his vocal cords to work around the emotions. Not that he could speak at the moment, but talking about personal relationships wasn't something he normally did. This was different, though. It was Eric.

And Miranda.

The woman he'd confided all his goals and aspirations to.

The only woman he'd given his heart to.

She dropped the cat onto the floor and moved to the couch, not quite touching him, but close enough her fragrance surrounded him, seeping into every ounce of his being, soothing him. Much as it had done last night. One part of him wanted to reach out, to touch her. The other part knew that was the last thing he should do, so he kept his hands firmly clasped between his knees.

"Want to tell me about him? Sometimes it helps to talk things out."

Incredulous, he turned his head and looked at her. Seriously? She expected him to open up to her about Eric? Wade struggled to regain his sense of cold, detached objectivity. It was the way he'd lived for years...the only way he knew how to exist. After several long moments, where she patiently and silently waited him out, he simply shook his head.

She gave him a slight nod, then sat back against the cushions. The cat had settled in her chair and, apparently, she was disinclined to disturb the feline.

Miranda looked totally relaxed, while Wade's body was wound tight as a bow string.

Without looking at her, he said, "It has been a long time."

She didn't pretend to not know what he was referring to. "Yes, it has," she said quietly.

"Why did you leave after I went to South America?" he accused. He hadn't wanted to lead off with that question, but it popped out. At times, it was best to simply go with your gut and not any preplanned interview. Except this wasn't an interview. It was simply discussing their past.

Wasn't it?

****

Randi stiffened, not liking his tone. "I beg your pardon. I don't know what you're talking about."

"Are you telling me you didn't go into hiding? You didn't turn your back on me, on our love, the minute I left?" His jaw worked back and forth.

She gasped. He couldn't have hurt her more if he'd physically slapped her. The words were like daggers piercing her heart. "How can you ask me that? Why would you even *think* it?"

"How long did you wait, Miranda?" Anger, and hurt, laced his words. "A day, a week? A whole month? Were you glad to be rid of me?"

Stunned, she sat staring for long moments. She took a shuddering breath before she spoke. "I thought you knew me better than that."

"Yeah, well. I thought so, too. Until I returned and found out you'd left right after I did."

"It wasn't right away," she mumbled.

"Not according to my sources." His voice was once

again hard and cold.

"What source…? Wait. My mother?"

Wade tipped his head, his expression clouded. "She said…"

How could this have happened? "Oh, Wade. She'd say anything to hurt me. And you believed her?"

This was a nightmare. No wonder he'd been so cold with her. What a mess! She had no intention of telling him the whole truth, but he needed to understand, to have a clearer picture of what had motivated her to do the things she did, of what her life had been like. "I didn't have much choice. My parents threw me out."

"They *what*?" He almost came off the couch, his anger with her now directed toward her parents.

Picking at a thread on her sweater, she glanced at his face, then averted her gaze. She couldn't stand to see the expression etched in his features. "That's how I wound up living with Granny," she said. Sitting in granny's recliner gave her peace and strength at the same time. It made her feel close to the one person who had welcomed her, accepted her for who she was, for who she could become. Who she *had* become.

He got up and paced the floor before turning to her, his laser focused eyes drilling into her. "I can't believe this. How could they…?" He waved his hand in the air. "Never mind. So, you came to live with your grandmother. Did you ever tell me about her?"

She tucked a strand of hair behind her ear before meeting his gaze. "No."

"Why not?" Did the man ever talk in a normal tone? His intensity, even in a regular conversation, was unnerving.

She spoke softly, the reality still hard to verbalize. "Because I didn't believe she loved me, or that I was even worthy of love."

"Where did you get that from?"

She rolled her eyes, then snorted. "Oh, Mom and Ray. Told me Granny didn't want to see me and to not contact her."

He frowned. "Yet you still wound up here. How?"

Panic flashed across her mind a moment before she pressed her lips together and lifted her chin. "Before she booted me out the door, Mom gave me Granny's address and phone number, saying we deserved each other. She came and got me. That's when I found out she'd tried to get ahold of me numerous times, but Ray put a restraining order on her, saying she had tried to abduct me in the past."

"Seriously? That man was a manipulative, sorry piece of..." He cut himself off.

Randi appreciated Wade's indignation on her behalf. "The abduction stuff was all a lie, of course. Basically, he wanted to keep me from trying to get in touch with her. And she had no idea how bad it was, not that there was anything she could have done."

He tilted his head sideways, as if trying to put a puzzle together but was missing some pieces. This was probably how he went about solving his cases. "How bad was it, Miranda. I know they were controlling and overly religious."

She grimaced. "Oh, it was so much more than that."

"How?" Wade's voice had taken on a hard edge, and his brow had furrowed. She saw a deep-down intensity in his gaze that told her he was always on the side of right and justice in every issue. "Are they still alive?"

Cold seeped into her at the thought of the man who played the role of her father for the majority of her formative years. "Don't know—don't care. Ray Seavers made my life a living hell, all in the name of religion. He didn't believe in a loving God, only a vengeful one. And that's not right. No one should be able to treat a child the way he treated me."

"What about your mother?"

"She was almost as bad as him. She could've stepped in and put a stop to a lot of his abuse, but she never did."

Wade stiffened; his scowl deepened. "Did he beat you?"

An ironic smile played at her lips. "Oh, nothing so obvious. Some of the spankings were a little too hard, but nothing I couldn't take. No, dear ole Ray was an expert at verbal and emotional abuse."

"Why didn't you tell me any of this before? You never once let on they abused you."

The memories caused her stomach to curdle and a shiver slide down her spine. "You've never been in a situation like that. It's not something you talk about, and you work really hard to project a different image to the world. At first, I thought that was the way it was supposed to be. And all my life I'd believed it was my fault. Later, after I realized the truth, I was…" She couldn't meet his gaze.

"You were what?" he coaxed.

She turned her head before she spoke. "I was ashamed."

"Aw, Miranda. You should have told me."

She sat there for several long moments, hating the sympathy, and worse, pity, in his features. It took a moment to regain her voice, to speak around the pain that continued to plague her to this day. "There's no way you can casually tell someone, *anyone*, you're abused. Instead, you hide it and learn to live with it the best you can."

He nodded, as if he had an inkling of an idea what it had been like. "How do you deal with it now?"

"I don't," she simply said. "I've put it behind me and have moved on. You know what they say about old wounds. How time and distance heal. Blah, blah, blah."

"Are you? Healed?"

She studied him for a moment, then smiled sweetly.

He sat for a long while, staring at one of the pictures on the wall, as if absorbing everything. Finally, he faced her, his tone accusatory. "Still, you disappeared. And you can't deny you changed your last name...a name so common it's extremely hard to track."

Rolling her eyes, she sank back against the cushions. "Oh, Wade. I didn't change my name to keep from being found. I changed it to my real father's."

He closed his eyes and rubbed the bridge of his nose before he said, "Your real...? That was why I couldn't find you. I'd been looking for a Seavers."

"I always hated that name and the man it belonged to." Why would he even doubt her?

"You told me Ray wasn't your biological father, but you never told me about your real dad or his name."

"That's because I didn't remember it. I was so young when he and Mom split up the only thing I ever called him was Daddy. I didn't know his first name, much less his last. And of course Mom wouldn't tell me anything.

"I don't know why she got so much pleasure in isolating me from Dad's side of the family. Granny told me about him after I moved here. He'd been trying to get in touch with me for years, so once we finally connected, I changed my name to his." A dark shadow passed over her. "Not long after, he died of a heart attack."

Some of the tension seemed to ease from Wade's body; his voice becoming less gruff. "I'm sorry you didn't have more time with him."

Chapter Seven

"Thank you for saying that. I still miss him." The ache of her father's loss still clung to Randi. If only she'd had more time with him. But what time she did have had been wonderful. She finally, finally knew what a parent's love felt like. If she ever had another child, she had her father's examples to go by. To raise the child by.

That was a big if, though.

Suddenly, her throat felt as parched as if she'd been in the middle of the desert for a week. "Would you like something to drink?"

"Sure. Whatever you have."

To her surprise, he followed her to the kitchen. It didn't feel as uncomfortable as she'd have thought so she set two bottles of water on the table. Wade pulled out a chair and waited until she'd dropped down into the chair opposite him before he sat. He took a deep swig of water and she did the same, then silence filled the room. Even Sebastian had disappeared.

As she sat there looking at Wade, it didn't take much for her to visualize the young man from high school, the man who had professed his love, to be sitting in her kitchen as if he belonged there. As if he'd *always* belonged there. A part of her wished with all her heart it was still true. She remembered the time he'd laughed as a butterfly had landed on the tip of her nose and she'd crossed her eyes trying to see it, until it had flown away. Her heart fluttered at the memory.

They'd lost so much simply because he'd gone on that trip. But it had been important to him, so she'd reluctantly given her blessing. The urge to reach out and touch his arm, which was only inches away, was overwhelming. To see if the spark they'd always had was still there. He glanced up and she could've sworn she saw the same feelings, the same appreciation for her he'd once had.

Then it was gone.

She kept her hands clasped tightly around the bottle of water. Wishing for something that would never be was a waste of energy. He no longer had feelings for her, and certainly not the romantic kind.

"So. Um…" She struggled for a safe subject to discuss. From the moment she'd seen him through the fog yesterday morning to this very instant, she'd wanted to find out where he'd been all these years. Yet now that he was here, sitting in her cozy kitchen and exuding all his *maleness*, she hesitated.

Finally, she took a deep breath and plunged into the topic she'd been avoiding. He'd gotten his answers, now it was her turn. Even if it broke the peaceful quiet they shared, she had to know.

"You said you went to my parents' house when you got back, but why didn't you call me before then? Once you left, I never heard a word from you. It was as if that mission was all that mattered and you forgot all about me." It was hard to look him in the eye, but she refused to avert her gaze. She wanted him to know how much he had hurt her. It was time to clear the air…once and for all.

He turned his head, his body stiffened and his jaw worked back and forth. The openness from moments ago dissipated. He met her gaze, his eyes dark. "I *couldn't* call, Miranda, because I was being held prisoner in a guerilla camp." His tone was almost conversational.

She gasped as her hand flew to her throat. "What? No."

He continued in a flat monotone, as if he hadn't been affected by the experience, as if he'd recited the events so many times that by now it was simply by rote. Nothing personal. Just something that had happened and of no consequence. "There wasn't anyone to pay the ransom demand, but they kept me alive anyway. They found I was a useful slave who didn't give them any problems."

She stared, slack jawed. She tried to swallow the lump that had formed in her throat. "I—I didn't know."

He grunted.

"If I'd known, I'd have moved heaven and earth to get you out." With no money to her name, she didn't know how she would have accomplished the feat, but she would have tried. She met his gaze, hoping he'd believe her sincerity. "I never would have abandoned you, Wade. You know that, right?"

He sat silent for a long time, studying her, his lip curled.

How could he doubt her? But apparently, he did. "How long were you held?"

"Ten months, thirteen days. I can give the number of hours, too, if you'd like." He sneered, but not before she saw the pain in his eyes.

"How did you get free?"

He stood and paced across the room, staring out the window over the sink. Finally, he turned to her. "A mercenary, hired to free another captive, took me with them."

"Were there others? Surely they weren't left behind?" She couldn't imagine the horror's he'd experienced.

He paused, a haunted look in his eye. "No one else survived besides us."

Miranda blanched.

"I learned a lot while in that filthy camp...mainly to rely on myself. Except I always knew you'd be waiting for me. That's what gave me the strength to keep going all those months, to endure the beatings, the starvation. Then I came home and found you'd abandoned me and were gone."

Her heart wrenched as tears stung her eyes. "Oh, Wade. It wasn't—"

He shot her a glaring look before continuing. "I pretty much went to hell after that. I drifted around the country—went on a drinking binge. After a while, I realized I was only hurting myself so I cleaned myself up and joined the FBI. Now, I use the survival and hunting skills I'd learned the hard way to find and put away morally corrupt people like those who'd held me prisoner."

Narrowing his eyes, he added for emphasis, "I'm good at it, too."

"Wh-what do you mean?" she asked, afraid of what he'd say.

In a swift move, he closed the space that separated them, placed one hand on the back of her chair and the other on the table beside her, hemming her in. His breath whispered on her face, as anger flashed in his eyes.

"Anytime the FBI have a really dirty job, a job no one else wants or can stomach, they call me. Behind my back, people say I don't have a heart…that I don't give a damn. I don't get emotionally involved in a case. I do my job. I follow my instincts, and I'm usually right." His eyes were now hard, his voice cold.

She wasn't afraid—exactly.

"I can thank you for that, Miranda. You made me the man I am today." His face resembled a piece of granite.

Her pulse jumped. Her breathing became shallow. This wasn't the man she used to know and love. But then, with a certainty from deep inside, she knew he'd never hurt her; that she was safe with him. "I don't know who you are anymore, Wade. I'm not sure I want to know. You are what you are because you choose to be this way. You made the choice." Her throat tightened, making talking difficult.

The solid mass hovering over her was both terrifying and exciting. Unable to get away from him, her heart beat wildly. His jaw clenched and his nostrils flared as he pulled her out of the chair and against his chest. She had expected his grip to hurt, but he barely touched her now. The thought of walking away crossed her mind, but she couldn't force herself to move. His face was close, his blue eyes even darker.

"What choices did I have, Miranda? Did I have a choice when I was kidnapped, stuck in that hell-hole and struggling to stay alive from day to day? Did I have a choice about where you were when I came back?"

His accusatory glare cut her to the bone, and a tear of regret slid down her cheek.

"Don't you dare cry on me," he demanded. "Don't you act like you're sorry when I know you're not. Don't you—"

She reached up and pressed her lips to his. He groaned a second before he wrapped his arms around her in a crushing embrace.

She didn't know why she'd kissed him. Except the agony so evident on his face and in his voice ate at her...as if she were kissing the pain away. At the moment, though, she couldn't have said whether it was his pain, or hers.

His warm lips made her forget everything. She inched toward him. Cocooned in his arms filled an aching void that permeated all the way to her soul. Until that moment, she hadn't realized she even felt empty. But within his embrace she found new strength, and all that mattered was being in Wade's arms.

Where she belonged.

****

Wade pulled back and pressed his forehead to hers. "Dammit, Miranda." However, there was no heat in his words. All of his anger and resentment of her had vanished the instant her lips met his. What was he doing? He needed to get out of there. He dropped his arms and stepped away, then turned toward the door.

"Don't go." Her voice was low, pleading...husky with emotion.

With his back to her, he hung his head. "It's no good. There's too much between us." He took another step.

Her hand on his arm stilled him. "There doesn't

have to be."

Why did she have to be so beautiful? So enticing? His heart squeezed. The warmth of her house, of her, called to him in ways he'd thought long dead.

"Will you stay a little longer?"

He hesitated.

"Please?"

He refused to give in. It wasn't good for him, or even her. About to walk out the door, out of her life, he found himself saying the last thing he expected. "All right."

And then she was in his arms, kissing him as if they were still teenagers, as if the last nine years had never happened. As if they had a future together. He couldn't force himself to let go, to even *want* to let go.

So he didn't.

****

Waking in the predawn hours, Wade had a hard time believing he was in Miranda's bed…had spent the better part of the night making passionate love to her. His world had righted when he sank into her. This wasn't sex, this was making love, just like they had done before. Only this was oh so much better. He didn't think he'd ever get enough of her. Falling asleep in her arms erased all the pain from the past. He let the steel armor around his heart drop away, feeling as if he'd been born anew. He *was* new. And it felt incredible.

He smiled, the feeling almost foreign it had been so long. When was the last time he'd been this happy? Oh, yes. The night before he left on that ill-fated mission trip. The night he'd slept with Miranda. It was no wonder, being with her again brought back the same essence of belonging, of peace.

Of happiness.

He got up to go to the bathroom. After he finished, he stood in the doorway and studied her sleeping figure. This was all he'd ever wanted, to wake up next to her every morning. Now, here he was. His heart swelled to the point he thought it would explode from the joy. Granted, they needed to work things out, get to know each other again, but he had faith they could do that.

More importantly, he needed her in his life. He had always needed her. Being a change-of-life baby, neither his two older siblings nor his parents had paid him much attention, leaving him to his own devices most of the time. They didn't intentionally neglect him, just expected him to be older than he really was. At an early age, he'd learned to be self-sufficient. His family loved him, but even now didn't have a lot of time for him. That's why when he'd found Miranda, he felt at home. He belonged and was finally important to another human being.

It hadn't mattered to her that he was geeky. She also needed someone who cared and they had bonded...he'd thought for life. Then there was that nine-year break he'd rather not delve into. Now, simply being with her again made him weak in the knees. How had he lived all these years without her? Deep down he knew he was good at his job because of her but he'd never wanted to give her credit...only blame her. That was behind them, though. He had a new appreciation of the woman before him.

Visions of cuddling in bed late at night, his leg thrown over hers with her hand resting on his heart after they'd made love, discussing their hopes and dreams for the future danced through his mind.

There were so many things they'd missed out on, like the simple day-to-day activities. Having meals together, taking long walks hand-in-hand, her introducing him to country life, him showing her around the city, going to her art gallery openings, and him learning to ride a motorcycle. Wade thought he might enjoy riding on his own bike, letting her take the lead and admiring her backside, anticipating when they got home and she would ride him.

Watching her sleep, her auburn hair fanned out against the pillow, sent another surge of desire for her though his system. About to climb back into bed, intending to wake her to another round of love making, he noticed a white photo album on the dresser. Assuming it was pictures of her as a little girl, or with her grandmother, he picked it up and flipped it open.

The first picture was of Miranda lying in a hospital bed, looking much the same as when he'd left for Columbia...and she was holding a newborn baby. Every cell in his body crystalized to the point he felt as if he might shatter. She'd had a child? Why hadn't she mentioned this? His body shook as he flipped through the pages. Miranda was in a few of the shots, but most were of two people he'd never seen before, and a little girl. The pictures progressed from infant to child.

A child with dark hair and blue eyes...who looked remarkedly like him.

Anger spread through him like a blazing wildfire. She'd deliberately kept this from him...had kept *his child* from him!

"What the *hell*, Miranda?"

She jerked awake at his outburst; confusion written on her features. Her eyes flew wide at the sight of the album. Realization, then guilt, replaced the earlier expression. "Oh, no! Wade. I can explain..." She jumped out of bed and reached for the book, which he kept out of her grasp.

He wasn't sure he could speak and clenched his back teeth together. His first instinct was to lash out. If she'd been a man, Wade would've let his fists do the talking. As it was, he couldn't, or rather wouldn't, touch her. He didn't hit women, even if they deserved it.

She kept looking from him to the album, then finally lowered her head before she pulled on a robe and sat on the end of the bed. Was she feeling regret he'd found out? Probably. Sleeping with him the night before had all been a ploy. One that had backfired on her. What else was she keeping from him?

Waving the book in front of her, he simply said, "Why? Why didn't you tell me?"

She didn't meet his gaze. "You have to understand—"

"All I understand is this—" he waved the book again for emphasis "—is the first thing you should have told me. Did you? No! Instead, you lured me into your bed. Was it a miscalculation on your part I even found this?"

Turning her head to the side, she bit her lower lip. "That's what I thought." The cold hatred for her he'd nursed for years slammed back into place with a resounding thud. This time, nothing would break that armor again. He had been a fool, falling for her lies, letting her sidetrack him. The woman was an expert at deception.

He thought they'd had a connection, that there was

hope for them after all. What a fool he'd been. He'd let his old feelings for her blind him and he'd lost his objectivity. But now he knew he had a daughter, and nothing under the sun would keep him from finding her. He'd lost eight years of her life, and he didn't intend to lose anymore.

"Wade, you have no idea what it was like, what I went through." Tears tracked down her cheeks unchecked.

Whatever she'd endured was nothing compared to the hell he'd been forced to live. Oh, she'd had a choice all right, and she'd chosen to give his baby away, to give their love for each other away. If it weren't for the firepit of hatred and betrayal smoldering inside him, he'd feel dead. As if he were back in that jungle, only this time he'd given up and hadn't survived. "Where is she, Miranda? Where's my daughter?"

She clamped her lips together and shook her head defiantly.

"Fine. I'm pretty sure I can find something in here, that will lead me to her." He held the photo album in front of her, just out of her reach. Teasing her; taunting her.

This time, there was a stricken look on her face. "No. You can't."

"You forget, I have resources and I'll use them to track her down." He didn't tell her using those resources for personal use was against policy, but he'd find a way around it if necessary. "She's *my* daughter!"

"And mine! But you can't rip her away from her parents. Do you want to destroy them? I love that child more than you can imagine, and have from the moment I found out I was pregnant." She paused and swallowed hard. "I miss her every single day, and wish more than anything I had her with me, but you can't uproot her life. It's the only home she has ever known. It's the best place for her, Wade."

What she said held a ring of truth to it, but he wasn't ready to listen to reason. Instead of arguing with her, he found his jeans and tugged them on. Where were his shoes? And socks? His shirt had to be here somewhere. Or was it in the hall? He'd been in such a rush to get her into bed, he wasn't sure where he'd left any of his clothes. Dammit. Why did this woman affect him this way? Part of him wanted to crawl back into bed with her, to lose himself in her like he'd done last night. The other part never wanted to see her again. Finally clothed, he strapped on his gun and walked out of the room, taking the album with him.

"Wade? Wade!" She rushed after him.

Her pleas didn't slow him down. After what she'd done, he would never trust her again. Nor would he listen to anything she had to say. Unless she wanted to give him his little girl's name and where to find her. He slammed the front door so hard it rattled the windows. Wade never wanted to hit somebody so badly in all his life. Where was a bad guy when you needed him? Or a good punching bag?

****

Heartbroken, Randi had spent hours crying, the warm glow from their lovemaking had long since faded. After years of longing, she had her one true love back in her life, only to have him walk out in a rage. A rage that wouldn't be easily pacified. She didn't blame him. If she'd just learned of the existence of her baby for the first time, she'd try to find her, too. As it was, the child was well cared for and loved. How to convince Wade of that and to leave her alone, though? No solution came to mind. Was there one? From what she'd seen, once he set his mind to something, he wouldn't stop until he achieved his goal.

Finally, she decided to spend the rest of the day painting. That was her go-to activity whenever anything was bothering her. Today, however, it hadn't worked. After going through several canvases, with none of the artwork looking remotely like her signature style— could have been painted by a talentless hack, in fact— she had given up.

Even Sebastian, who always kept her company while she worked, had scurried away after she'd thrown a botched canvas across the room. Yes, it was childish, but she'd felt marginally better afterward. At that point, she'd given up, leaving the discarded canvas where it lay in the corner. She had taken refuge in the recliner and turned on the TV…not paying much attention to what was on.

As the day wore on, she noticed sounds of trucks leaving—more voices closer to the house for a while— then silence. Almost dark, she walked out on her front porch. The Red Cross tent was gone, along with the people. No vehicles were in sight and no noise of any kind coming from the crash site.

The NTSB had finished their cleanup and left, which meant Wade was also gone…for good this time. A physical ache so deep she lost her breath speared her. She hadn't thought her heart could ache any more than when he'd stormed out of her house earlier.

She'd been wrong. A large piece of her had gone with him. Now, here she stood.

Alone.

Again.

The last time he'd left, and after she'd given up the baby, she'd had Granny to prop her up—to give her a reason to keep going. Now, she had no one. Sebastian rubbed against her legs, reminding her of his presence. At least there was still one being who needed her. She bent down and hefted him into her arms.

"Come on, sweetie. Let's get a bite to eat. Maybe some special chow for you and some ice cream for me." And maybe a pitcher of margaritas to go along with it.

A half hour later, she pulled on her old work jacket and went out to the back porch, Sebastian trailing behind. The air was cool and bit at her nose, but she didn't care. Anytime she was upset, she'd come out here and soak in the wonders of Mother Nature.

Bypassing the small table and chairs near the door, she sank down onto one of the wide porch steps and poured herself a drink. The last time she'd sat out here, Wade had found her and then someone had taken a shot at them.

She snorted. Let the shooter come back and put her out of her misery. She wasn't worried about a recurrence, though. Everyone was gone. There was no reason for anyone to still be hanging around—yet, with the silence came a spooky feeling. The quiet was unnerving as a shiver slid down her back. How had she gotten so used to the noise in only a couple of days? Even Sebastian noticed as he peered out into the forest, to where men and machines had been constantly going. Finally, the cat lay curled at her side as she sipped her drink, relishing the taste. She needed to slip into oblivion and drown out the realities of the last few days.

She heard rustling from the bushes and peered intently into the darkness. Nothing. Probably a deer. "Same ole, same ole," she told herself. Still, she griped the glass a little tighter and was entertaining the idea of going back inside and locking the door when she heard it again. Sebastian perked up, also. Someone *was* out there.

"Who...who's there?"

No response.

She jumped to her feet—intent on going inside. Sebastian chose that moment to skitter off the porch.

"I'm sorry, ma'am. I didn't mean to startle you," came a kind voice as a man emerged from the darkness and stepped into the light.

She stopped, still leery. "Who are you?" No one should be here. Perhaps she needed to put a No Trespassing sign at the end of her property. Now that the authorities were gone, gawkers like this guy would probably show up.

"Oh, I'm an acquaintance of your boyfriend," he said as he moved closer.

"My boy—. You mean Wade? Hate to disappoint you, but he isn't my boyfriend." Not now, anyway. "Do you work with him?"

He let out a short laugh. "Naw, we don't work together. But we have a history of sorts."

Of sorts? What did that mean? "He's not here right now, but I expect him at any minute," she said as she edged up onto the next step and closer to the door. The stranger gave off the appearance of being harmless, but the quiet of the night reminded her of how vulnerable she was. Hairs stood up on the back of her neck. The shotgun and wasp spray were in her bedroom. Too far away. She needed to have something between her and him—preferably a locked door. Maybe she could casually move and get inside without seeming to be rude. Her ingrained manners prevented her from turning her back on him and bolting. He hadn't given her any reason to be suspicious.

He stopped just short of the porch steps, his hands in the pockets of his jacket. "Yes, he'll be along shortly."

Randi's alarm bells went off. He was trying to present a casual stance, but wasn't quite achieving the effect. There was something about him that was familiar, but she couldn't put her finger on it. She had seen him somewhere. But where? She took another step back. She inhaled sharply as she gripped the handrail. "Wh-what do you want? What are you doing here?"

He tilted his head back and laughed a shrill high-pitched laugh. The laugh of a mad man. Icy fingers of dread crept down her spine. She was alone. If she screamed, there wasn't anyone to hear. *Run!* every fiber of her being yelled. She turned to dash for the door and in her haste knocked the pitcher over, spilling the liquid across the steps.

Distracted, she didn't notice him moving. In a flash, he bounded up the steps and grabbed her arm. The next instant, he covered her mouth with a cloth. Her stomach rolled as a sweet, sickening smell gagged her. *No-o-o.*

Darkness overtook her.

Chapter Eight

A black cloud hung over Wade's head. Miranda gave my child away, echoed through his mind, over and over...like a broken record stuck in the same spot. It felt as if a white-hot poker had pierced the core of his being. He couldn't think...couldn't breathe. He'd left her house for her own safety, not sure if he'd be able to contain his fury.

The worst part? He'd come to accept her and had let her back into his heart. Startling, considering his feelings when he'd first seen her three days ago. Three days. Was that all it had been? Since he'd first learned of Eric's death and stepped off the plane on Arkansas soil, he had been on an emotional rollercoaster.

He still had responsibilities, though, and had spent a large portion of the day with Agents Wesson and Smith. Containing his rage and not letting it interfere with his job had been difficult. The three agents had gone back to the house and walked the area again for any signs they might have missed the day before. Wade held his breath, hoping Miranda wouldn't come outside. He wasn't sure he could stand to see her, not this soon after learning of her deception.

She hadn't. So why did a part of him feel cheated?

Using the conference room at the sheriff's office as a base, the agents went over the ballistics from the bullet fragment. They identified the caliber of weapon, but not much else. No prints were on the bullet or the casing found the day before. The scrap of clothing was also a dead end, though they hadn't given up. The most unsettling thing was not knowing why Wade had been shot at. Who in the area knew him? Smith and Wesson would undoubtably go over all of Wade's old cases, looking for anyone who might be connected to this region. They agreed he should return to the home office and let the other two agents take over the case.

Sheriff Bennett stood in the open doorway. "Anything I can do to help?" He had dealt with the FBI before and understood his role in the investigation. Or lack thereof. His job was to assist, nothing more.

Agent Smith turned to him. "Not at this time, but we appreciate your assistance. Glad you stopped by, though. The FAA and NTSB have determined the cause of the crash."

Bennett tensed, as did Wade. They hadn't shared that piece of info with him, either.

"The fog was a contributing factor, but there were also some mechanical issues."

"So, no bomb and not a pilot error," the sheriff stated.

"If there hadn't been the low visibility, the pilots might have been able to correct the issue enough to get to the airport. As it was, they didn't know what was coming at them until it was too late." Smith looked as grim as Wade felt.

Lines bracketed Bennett's mouth. "Damn."

"I'll second that," Wade added. The lives lost was senseless. The plane going down hadn't been an act of terrorism, just an accident. An accident that had brought him face to face with his past.

Fool that he was, he'd let himself believe there could be something between them again. But those hopes went up in flames as soon as he'd found out what she'd done. The rage burning just beneath the surface made it difficult to breathe. He needed to get as far away from here as possible. The sooner the better.

He darted a quick glance at the large clock on the wall—almost seven. He had intended to be out of town by now, but the investigation with the other two agents had taken longer than he'd expected. "Wesson, do you and Smith have all the information you need?"

"We can handle it from here, Malone," Agent Wesson replied. "If we have any more questions, or if we find something pertinent, we know where to find you." A man of few words, and a preference for the old-fashioned way of taking notes, he flipped his notebook closed and neatly tucked it into his suit pocket. He rose at the same time Agent Smith did. They shook hands with the sheriff and left.

"They don't say much, do they?" Jake asked.

"No, but they're good. They remind me of bloodhounds. They put their noses down and don't look up till they've caught the bad guys. If whoever did the shooting the other night is still around, those two will find him."

"They're that good, huh?"

"Yeah, together, they're even better than me," Wade said with a wry grin. He made a point of looking at the clock again. His skin itched to get on the road. "Time I got going."

Jake shook his hand. "Good working with you, Malone."

Wade nodded and they left the building, then parted ways in the parking lot. Jake got into his patrol car, and Wade took his time getting into his rental. He slid behind the wheel, then turned the Ford Escort in the direction of the motel. All he had to do was collect his bag, check out, then put as many miles as possible between himself and Miranda.

She had subtly snuck back into his heart and he'd allowed himself to fall under her spell. But the fact she'd deliberately deceived him made him more bitter than he'd been since—well, since he'd learned she'd left him. You can't change a leopard's spots, he thought. The shell he'd built around himself reemerged and he vowed never to let anyone get close to him again. Ever.

He pulled into the parking space in front of his motel room, the room he had yet to sleep in, still contemplating what to do with the newfound knowledge of his parentage. Leaving the motel behind wouldn't hurt his feelings any. He'd stayed in worse, but much preferred his townhouse back in Kansas City. Who could sleep with all the quiet around here, anyway? In the city there was always traffic and some sort of noise. The peacefulness of the Ozarks allowed thoughts to creep into his brain the city noise kept at bay during the long nights.

Yes, he was looking forward to going back to the townhouse. Odd, he always thought of where he lived like that, and never as home. The image of a home brought to mind Miranda's house. *No. I won't go there.* He pushed the thought from his head.

Distracted, he climbed from the car, unlocked the motel door, pushed it open…

And froze.

Then, with an instinct long practiced, his gun was out of the holster and in his hand in a flash as he took in the ransacked room. It didn't look like the perpetrator was still there, but he moved cautiously all the same. Anything that could be turned over had been...the chair, table, lamps, pillows, bedding, and the contents of his suitcase. All scattered in an almost deliberate pattern. Then he saw the writing on the broken mirror. His blood ran cold as he stared at the message.

COME ALONE OR SHE DIES

He shoved the gun back into the holster and ran for his car. A small part of his brain said to call his fellow agents, but for the first time in years, panic overwhelmed him, blocking all rational thought from his mind.

His tires squealed on the pavement as he backed out of the parking space, and all the while he berated himself. What had he done? What signs and clues had he overlooked? If Miranda had been hurt because of him, he'd never forgive himself. He still hated her for what she'd done, but she was in trouble because of him. Unacceptable. He scrubbed a hand over his face as sweat popped out on his forehead.

A sickening feeling lay in his stomach. A sense of urgency caused him to drive faster than was prudent. Would he be in time to save her? Dread engulfed him.

Your fault—your fault, played through his mind as he sped toward Miranda's home.

****

The house was dark as Wade coasted to a stop. He didn't see any cars around except Miranda's, but that didn't mean anything. He eased from the car, gun in hand, and cautiously made his way to the front door. Locked. He moved around the side of the dark house to the back. The porch light was all that was on. He stood in the shadows a moment, trying to get a sense of anyone's presence, but the only sounds came from the tree frogs and crickets.

Satisfied, he moved up the steps to the open door. On his way, he saw an overturned pitcher and broken glass. That could have been staged, or be what it looked like. Someone had startled her as she sat there. His heart tripped once before he reeled it in, refusing to let his emotions get involved. Only his years of training and experience could save her now.

He slipped inside, hugging the walls. The house was dark, so he pulled a small flashlight out of his pocket and scanned the kitchen. The countertop was a mess where she had made her drink. His heart thudded. Twenty-four hours ago he'd sat in this room and they had confided in each other...had cleared the air and reconnected. At least he'd thought so. Then he discovered the one thing she had conveniently forgotten to reveal. The most important bit of news that changed his life. Pain from her betrayal gripped him. No. He refused to go there. Not now. He'd deal with that issue later. This time he physically shook his head to dispel any emotions or wayward thoughts. He needed to focus.

He didn't want to turn on any lights and attract attention, or alert the kidnapper he was there, so with the narrow beam of light, made his way from one room to the next. Nothing inside the house was out of place. Obviously, Miranda had been abducted while she sat on the porch.

Wade left by the front door and worked his way to

the back again. A full moon had risen, but he stayed in the shadows, searching for signs. While in the jungle, he'd learned by opening himself up, he could sense things he might not notice otherwise. Squatting, he closed his eyes and breathed deeply. A faint hint of an odd odor drifted around him.

Without looking, he reached down and his fingers struck a small container lying next to a tree. Waving the scent toward his nose, the smell was unmistakable — chloroform. That was how Miranda had been taken without much of a fight. And he was sure the woman would have given the kidnapper a hard time of it. Rising, he studied the area. Where had he taken her? Wade moved back to the porch, trying to get a feel for what had taken place.

At the bottom step he sat on his haunches and studied the ground. Slight indentations in the grass, where someone had walked, were still visible. Either the man was extremely large, or he was carrying something heavy. Miranda. The tracks led into the woods. As he was about to stand, he sensed movement behind him.

He whirled, gun ready. Miranda's cat, Sebastian, sat looking at him, then opened its mouth as if it were talking, but no sound came out. The feline stared him in the eye while its tail twitched in agitation. What was going on with it?

He absently stretched his hand toward Sebastian's head, only to have the animal back away from him. Dismissing the cat, he rose and headed in the direction the kidnapper had gone. Pausing at the tree line, he noted the cat directly behind him, staring into the dense foliage. As Wade moved into the woods, the feline padded silently along a couple paces behind him. If the cat didn't get in his way, he would tolerate its presence. Besides, how did anyone tell a cat to stay home? Wade almost snorted. This one in particular had a mind of his own.

****

Randi's head pounded and felt as if it was about to split open, so she tried not to move. What had happened? The last thing she remembered was a stranger. He attacked her. The sickeningly sweet odor of whatever he'd used to drug her still clung to her. Slowly she opened her eyes.

A lantern lit the area, revealing an old wooden beam that held up what was left of the rotted roof. Cobwebs hung from the sagging rafters. Her feet and hands were bound in front of her and she was lying on a musty dirt floor. The stench of moldy hay assailed her, causing her stomach to pitch.

She was in an old dilapidated, and drafty building. Thankfully, she still had on her jacket. Looking more closely, she realized it was the barn on the backside of her property. She hadn't been here in years, but she remembered Granny selling all the implements at a flea market not long after Randi moved in with her. *Rats.* She could have used one to cut herself loose.

Fighting the urge to throw up, she turned her eyes to the side at the faint sounds of movement. The man who'd abducted her. What was he doing? He didn't seem to know she was awake. If only her stomach would cooperate, maybe she could fake him out. She took a deep breath, but the musty smell only made matters worse. Unable to stop herself, she hastily rolled to her side, sat up on her knees and vomited.

With the contents of her stomach on the ground before her, and she'd caught her breath, Randi noticed the shoes in her line of vision. She spit one more time, trying to get rid of the last of the bile, and wiped her mouth on the sleeve of her jacket. She wished she had the courage to spit *on* his shoes, but she wasn't that brave. Obviously, he was a madman, and who knew what he was capable of?

"Who are you?" She didn't need to see his face to know what he looked like. She wouldn't allow herself to forget his features so she could describe him to a sketch artist. In fact, she'd draw him herself. One day, she vowed, she'd testify at his trial.

The only sound was his heavy breathing.

Anger flared in her. She tried to push herself to her feet, almost fell in the vomit and landed with a thump on her hip. "Ow!"

A laugh escaped him as he finally bent down to check the knots on her wrists. "You're not going anywhere, not before I want you to, anyway, so don't get excited."

Randi didn't know what to make of him. He'd drugged and kidnapped her, but he'd been fairly gentle while checking the ropes on her wrists and feet.

Maybe she could reason with him. "Listen, I can get you money. I'll go to the bank as soon as it opens tomorrow and withdraw everything I have. Just please don't hurt me."

He laughed again—that high shrill laugh she'd heard back at her house—so reasoning with him was out of the question. The man had lost his mind. Problem was, she was his captive. What did he have planned for her? She'd heard of women being abducted, raped and tortured for days before anyone found them.

She shuddered. No one would be looking for her. Not yet anyway. In the morning they might start to get curious about her, but she was a solitary person and, at times, went days without seeing anyone while she was working on a project. Melody would eventually check on her, but by then it'd be too late. That was the way it usually worked, wasn't it? In all the movies and TV shows she'd seen, the poor woman was found, but she was always dead.

Randi had to get loose, get away from him. But how?

He stood and headed toward the door.

"Wait!"

Turning only his head, he studied her with hooded eyes. "Too bad, pretty lady. You chose to keep the wrong company."

"I don't know who you're talking about. What company?" she pleaded frantically.

After watching her squirm against the ropes a little longer, he finally said, "Sure, you do. Your boyfriend."

Wade. She resisted the urge to roll her eyes. "I told you before, he's *not* my boyfriend. Get that through your thick skull."

"Ah, but he'll still come for you. Then you'll both die."

"No." The word came out on a gush of air as Randi stared at him in horror.

Abruptly, he snapped his fingers, then pivoted and went to the corner where he'd been before. When he faced her direction, he held some sort of device. Ignoring her, he casually walked out, pulling the rickety barn door closed behind him with an ominous thud.

For long moments, she continued to focus on the closed door. *This can't be happening. It has to be a horrible nightmare. I'm going to wake up soon and be home in my own bed. Sebastian will come clambering up on top of me, like he does every morning. I'll get up and burn the French toast, like I always do. Oh, please, let this be a dream!*

A sob escaped as her shoulders shook. Despite her best efforts, tears stung the back of her eyes, then flowed down her cheeks. She and Wade were going to die. The kidnapper had said so, and there was nothing she could do to stop it.

****

Phillip hid in the shadows of the trees—his fingers itching to press the button on the remote. *But not yet. Just a little longer and then it'll all be over.* His palms grew clammy as sweat dripped off his forehead. Absently, he rubbed his free hand down the leg of his pants, then switched the remote and did the same for the other hand. He was so close. He couldn't make any mistakes now. He didn't want to take the chance of his fingers slipping. It was imperative the timing be just right.

His entire world had come crashing down when his kid brother had been killed...by Malone, *a damn rookie*. Patrick was better than that—he deserved better.

Since they had been old enough to crawl, their old man had taught them the importance of discipline and how to be strong. Their mother never understood. She was weak. They had watched as she groveled at their father's feet. But she never learned. One day she simply disappeared. She hadn't been missed. Over the years, he'd wondered if his dad had killed her, but Phillip had never asked. In the end, it didn't matter.

As boys, he and Patrick had spent hours learning how to take care of themselves and each other. Their old man had seen to it his sons knew how to handle *any* situation, to not let anyone get the best of them. Lying, cheating, stealing, it was a way of life. Their old man was mean and tough. And he made his sons even tougher and meaner. It was a family tradition.

Patrick had been the perfect son. He had learned every dirty trick in the book, making him even more cunning than their father. He'd gotten into trouble, but then that was expected. However, when he attracted the attention of the Feds, things had started going wrong.

His little brother had managed to get out of jams even he would have given up on. But that time—the last time—he'd been cornered by the Feds and Patrick had shot one of them. Purely self-preservation, mind you.

Then they'd put out the story Malone had gotten the drop on him and taken him down. Ridiculous. No one was that good. Especially not a rookie on his first assignment. Malone must have bushwhacked the kid.

Every time he thought of Patrick, his stomach churned and acid burned his throat. The loss still hurt like a knife being twisted in his chest. Family was the most important thing in the world...the only ones who were dependable. The only ones who counted. Everyone else betrayed you in the end. Now he was alone. Both his father and brother were dead. But he was there to make sure Patrick's murderer got what was coming to him. No decent brother would do differently.

Yes, Phillip had made it his business to learn everything possible about the now infamous Agent

Malone and track his career. It was fate they'd both wound up on this mountaintop at the same time. Now it was payback time.

Movement through the trees caught his attention. *Yes! Finally. It's about time you showed up.* Leaning farther into the shadows, he watched as Malone came into view, then stopped. Phillip's heart beat a fast-staccato rhythm as he held his breath. He could hardly contain his excitement. *Come on. What are you waiting for?* Drawing his brows together, he willed the fed to move toward the barn.

Patience was not one of his strong suits. That was why Patrick had been better at everything. The kid would sit for hours in almost the same position, just to get the drop on someone. Unable to do the same, Phillip's will power was almost at an end when Malone finally ducked behind a tree.

The lantern burned in the barn, so light slid underneath the door and seeped through the rotting cracks in the boards. *He's seen it, but he's cautious—I can appreciate that. But get moving! I haven't got all night.*

To his chagrin, Malone didn't move to the barn. Instead, he stayed clear of the building and circled around the back—and out of his sight. *I'll wait you out. There's no other way in except this one. And when you get to the door, I want you to see who's inside. Then you're both history.*

Irritated, he glanced at his watch, only to realize he couldn't read the dial, even with the full moon shining through the trees. Taking a deep breath, he leaned against the large tree he'd chosen as a shield from the upcoming blast and concentrated on the other side of the building. The side that should reveal Malone after he'd made his circle. He was getting giddy with the thought of what was to come.

Any minute now. Any minute.

****

Slowly, a pungent odor penetrated Randi's senses, breaking the hysteria she'd been in. She lowered her gaze to where she had thrown up a short while earlier, her nose wrinkling at the awful smell. Her stomach pitched again, but she was able to tamp down the urge to release what was left of its contents. Her brow knit into a frown.

What was she doing simply sitting there waiting for the inevitable? She brushed the remaining tears away with the back of her hand, the rough rope chaffing where it made contact with her cheek. Surely there was a way out of this. All she had to do was find it.

Glancing at the door, then to the corner where the kidnapper had been standing when she'd come to, she saw an object lying in the hay. What was it? If only she could get out of these ropes. She took a deep breath, then almost gagged at the stench. *Ooh, bad idea.*

Rolling on her side, away from the vomit, she came back to a sitting position. Maybe she could use her yoga training. Twisting every way she knew, she still wasn't able to free even one of her hands. But she was able to move so she started scooting toward the back of the barn. Searching the walls for anything she could use to cut the ropes, she continued until she was at the far back stall. If nothing else, maybe she could find a loose board and get out, even if she was still tied up.

Then she saw it. Lying in the corner, with little more than the handle showing through the pile of old hay, was a hand saw. *Bless you Granny for leaving this here.* After she'd reached the saw, she propped her feet against the stone foundation and, pulling her feet as far apart as possible to put pressure on the ropes, started hacking at them with the rusty saw teeth. Finally, her feet broke free.

Without skipping a beat, she placed the handle of the saw between her feet, braced the flat of the blade against the thick coat on her stomach and began working on the ropes around her wrists. Several times the blade slipped and she nicked her skin. Ignoring the sting, she kept working frantically. *Come on, come on!* In her mind she heard the clock ticking. Then—the last of the now tattered rope gave way.

Heaving a sigh of relief, she rubbed her wrists then shook them to regain the blood flow. They were raw, but they'd heal along with the nicks—if she lived. Keeping an eye on the door, she crept over to the corner…she had to see what the man was so interested in. Her heart pounded against her ribcage as she realized what was there; dynamite, with a timer attached.

Her stomach churned as ice water flowed through her veins, immobilizing her. She was the bait.

Somehow, he was luring Wade to the barn. But why kill him? "The man's out of his mind. It doesn't matter why," she muttered to herself. Wade had to be warned, to be stopped, before it was too late. Once he set foot inside the structure, they would die.

That thought brought her out of her paralyzing fear, and she looked for a way out. Using the door as a means of escape was obviously out of the question. Unsure how long she might have before Wade showed up, she frantically looked around the old building for a way out. Pushing gingerly against the boards on the back wall, Randi finally found one rotted loose. She clenched her teeth with each creak of the board as she worked it free from the rusted nail holding it in place. Maybe the kidnapper was far enough away he wouldn't hear the noise and realize what she was doing. It was dumb on his part to have left her conscious, anyway. Perhaps he was overconfident, but one thing was for sure, he had sorely underestimated her.

Shoving harder, she tumbled outside as the board gave way.

Chapter Nine

Wade tried his best to stay in the shadows, but the moon teased him at every step. He hated working during a full moon. It destroyed a lot of his cover. And tonight, it was so bright it almost beckoned him to reach up and touch it. A Swiss cheese kind of moon. A romantic moon, he mused. Deliberately, he pulled his gaze away from the sky and back to the woods. There was work to do. Miranda's life depended on him, and he was determined to not let anything happen to her.

Once he'd seen the barn, he'd known she was inside. It was so obvious. The trail led right to the structure, the light inside. It all but shouted—*she's here. Come and get her.* That was why he chose to steer clear of the building until he cased it. Until he found a way to get her away safely.

Using his years of training, he quietly worked through the dense foliage and made his way around the side of the building. Once behind it, he stopped. A slight noise caught his attention, a sound that didn't blend in with the other sounds of the night. Easing closer, he discovered it was coming from inside the structure. Someone was moving one of the boards, working it free from the studs. If the kidnapper was trying to sneak out, then he'd made a major mistake. *I've got you now.*

Gun raised, he eased along the side of the barn and waited. Every muscle in his body tensed. All his energy focused as he anticipated taking the perpetrator down. Pointing the gun at the head that appeared through the opening, he sucked in a deep breath when he recognized the mop of hair. Miranda.

Smiling to himself, he had to admire her. Looked as if she didn't need rescuing after all. As he waited for her to crawl out, he enjoyed the view of her shapely posterior as it stuck up in the air. She straightened and he moved close behind her and let her back into him, enjoying the feel of her. He did not, however, enjoy the elbow she drove into his ribs with a force that took his breath away.

Then she stomped on his foot with her heel, sending a sharp pain up his leg. He wrapped his arms around her to keep her from doing him any more harm. At this rate, he would be the one needing to be rescued. Maybe he shouldn't have surprised her, he thought as he placed his hand over her mouth before she screamed.

"Miranda. It's me," he whispered into her ear.

At the sound of his voice, she whirled and stared into his eyes. Relief flooded her face and she flung her arms around his neck. "Oh, Wade…"

Wrapping her in a bear hug, he kissed the top of her head. "It's all right." He had her in his arms, amazed at how much he'd missed her, and basked in the feel of her body against his.

The smell of dirt, decayed hay, and vomit, mingled with her almond shampoo as he buried his face in her hair. He'd almost lost her. As the thought gripped him, he pulled her even closer. Now that she was out of the barn, he could get her to safety. *Then* he'd deal with the kidnapper.

Suddenly she lifted her head, a panicked look on her face. "Oh, we've got to go. We've got to go *now!*"

"What?" Hairs on the back of his neck stood on end.

"A bomb."

All thought of holding her vanished. "Where?" he demanded.

Jerking on his arm, she said, "In the barn. He was waiting for you. He planted a bomb."

Heart pounding, Wade grabbed her hand as together they dashed toward the shelter of the woods. *If we can get into the tree line, we'll have some cover. Just a few more yards. Then maybe we can—*

Caught by the force of the explosion, they were propelled forward off their feet. Unable to shield Miranda from hitting the hard ground, he rolled over her to shield her as burning debris from the building showered down around them.

Boards, pieces of metal and hot embers fell on them as he covered her. The debris, as it hit him, didn't hurt too much, thank goodness. Were they going to luck out and get off without any real injuries? As soon as the thought filtered through his head, a sharp object pierced his calf and sent pain soaring up his leg. He stifled a curse under his breath, but he didn't move. Not until he was sure she wouldn't be hit.

Finally, he moved away from her and looked at the remains of the barn. Not much was left, and what still stood was a raging inferno. It wouldn't be long before nothing was left but ashes. For the time being, though, they still had a little cover. "Are you all right?" he asked.

"Uh, yes, I think so." The words came out more of a croak as she struggled to sit up. She dusted glowing embers off his back then her slacks. "Do you think he'll—"

Fuzzy blackness threatened to engulf him. Searing pain shot up his leg and he was having muscle spasms that rivaled any Charlie Horse he'd ever had, so he took deep breaths as he waited out the worst of it. *Move past the pain. You've done it a dozen times before. You can do it again. Concentrate!* He shifted his attention to the boards littering the area, to the heat from the burning structure…anything but the pain that gripped him. If he lost consciousness, he wouldn't do either of them any good. Gradually, Miranda's voice registered in his brain.

"Wade? Did you hear what I said?" She laid a hand on his shoulder as she spoke.

"Hmm?"

"Do you think he'll come looking for us?"

"Oh, uh, yeah." *Focus!* "Do…do you know who he is?"

"He looked familiar, but I can't remember from where. Even though I don't know him, he sure knows you. This was all set up as a trap to kill you." She glanced toward the burning structure and visibly shuddered. "We were supposed to be in there."

Wade twisted around and looked at her. "Then I was the target all along. Sorry to have gotten you into this. If I'd known, I would have—"

"But you didn't know." She met his gaze squarely, apparently undaunted.

He berated himself for sloppy work. Being distracted by her was no excuse. "He's probably the one who shot at us the other night and it was my job to find out. But I didn't, and it almost got us killed. Twice."

"I don't blame you, Wade. I blame *him.*" She jerked her head toward the demolished barn.

"Yeah, well, it's time we got moving." He tried to rise, then, as pain cramped his leg, he dropped back to the ground. This time he couldn't stifle the curse.

"What is it?" Concern etched in her voice.

He yanked a handkerchief out of his pocket and leaned over his leg, then tied the cloth over the brightly flowing stream of blood coming from his calf. Giving the makeshift bandage an extra tug, he grunted.

Miranda sucked in a harsh breath. "You're hurt!"

"It's nothing. Help me up," he ground out through the pain. He'd endured worse while a captive, but it had been a long time since then. Over the years he'd gotten soft. Or at least used to *not* having to experience pain so intense it took your breath away.

She didn't look convinced, but silently stood and, bracing her feet, took hold of his hand with both of hers. Leaning backwards, she allowed him to pull himself up, using her for leverage. He draped his arm around her shoulders as if she were a crutch.

"Are you sure you can do this?" he asked.

"I can if you can," she said grimly. "Besides, what choice do we have?"

He shook his head, then pulled his cell phone out of his pocket, but then frowned.

She looked at the phone and sighed. "I was afraid of that. It's hard to get cell coverage out here sometimes."

"Great," he muttered as he shoved the phone back in his pocket.

"Sorry. The 'joys' of living in the mountains."

"You know, you *could* leave me here and go for help."

Her expression suggested he'd grown two heads. "Look, there's no way I'd go off and leave you when you can't even walk by yourself. What type of person do you think I am? Besides, that guy is still out there and I don't want to run into him again. Once was more than enough."

Wade glared at her—*stubborn woman!*—and she glared right back. His admiration for her went up a notch. Pulling his gaze away, he studied the terrain and tried to get a feel for where they were.

"Okay, macho man, let's get going."

Stealing a glance, he found her eyes dancing with laughter. Stubborn, but tough. Serious, but lighthearted. He hoped she had enough grit to face what was still ahead. "Do you have any idea where we are?"

"We're on the backside of my property, but I haven't been out here in a long time."

Grateful she intended to stick it out, he jerked his head toward the thick foliage. Leaning heavily on her, they headed away from the blazing heat...and the kidnapper.

****

The explosion was magnificent! Everything Phillip had expected—and more. The tree he'd hid behind had taken the brunt of the blast, but he still had to duck the flying debris. When it was painfully apparent Malone wasn't going to come back to the front of the barn, he'd figured the fed had either found another way in or kept moving. In any case, he couldn't take any chances on Malone or his girlfriend getting away.

As the ringing stopped in his ears, Phillip peered around. Fire raged as the ancient wood popped and crackled before succumbing to the intense heat. *Such a beautiful sight. Nothing's more glorious than the total destruction of a building...except to see someone you hate take their last breath.* He took a moment to simply enjoy his handiwork, satisfaction rippling through him.

With a sigh, he stood, pondering whether or not his mission was actually accomplished. Had he finally avenged his brothers' death? Speculating Malone was either in the building or near enough to have been killed wasn't good enough. He had to have proof. Had to be sure. Taking a wide berth, he circled the remains of the barn, keeping a careful eye out for human movement.

By the time he'd gotten to the back of the burning building, he'd almost convinced himself there was no way Malone could have survived the explosion, even though he hadn't found a body yet. Maybe there wasn't one. Maybe he'd been close enough to have simply been blown apart. That'd be perfect. A smile played across his lips at the thought. But it'd be nice to find some body parts.

Stepping gingerly, he noticed a slightly different pattern to the debris littering the ground. He glanced around for a possible ambush, then moved closer. Yes, someone had lain there when the barn came down. Malone. He judged the distance from the barn and, since there was no body, figured the fed had been far enough away to have survived.

A dark spot drew his attention. He squatted and studied the area, touched a blade of grass with the tip of his finger. *Ah, blood. He's hurt.* And from the looks of the stain, it's bad. *Yes. This isn't over yet, Malone.* He pushed to his feet and studied the area closer. *Which way did you go?*

There was still plenty of light from the fire, so it wasn't long before he was able to discern two sets of footprints. One much smaller than the other. *Hell, how'd the stupid woman get out? I had her hogtied.*

He ground his teeth together. At the very least, *she* should've been dead. She'd still die, though. Except now Malone could watch her die a more painful death. Right before Malone himself got what he had coming.

Tracking them was going to be simple. After he figured out the general direction they'd headed, it was easy to see their path. The brush was trampled and there was a lot of blood. Once in the woods, he wouldn't be able to see the blood, but it looked as if one of them was dragging a leg. Most likely Malone from all appearances. *Good. That will make this even more fun.*

A glint among the debris caught his eye as he turned to follow them. Squinting, his eyes widened as he bent to retrieve the object. *Well, well, well. Seems lady luck has decided to smile on me after all.* Unable to contain himself, he threw his head back and roared with laughter, not caring if he was heard or not.

In his hand lay Wade Malone's gun. Probably the same gun that had killed Patrick. This revenge would be even sweeter.

****

Brambles snagged Randi's pants. If not for the old denim jacket, her arms would have been ripped and torn in a hundred places. Wade's lightweight jacket and blue jeans afforded him a small measure of protection. She desperately wished for her own jeans and boots. Her thin slacks and tennis shoes weren't doing her any favors.

Adrenaline gave her extra strength. Initially. They had settled into a pattern of sorts, stumbling every now and then over the rough terrain. But for the most part, they'd developed a rhythm that allowed them to make some progress, putting some distance between them and the fire. And the kidnapper. As they continued to plod along, exhaustion slowly settled in. Wade was doing his best to hold his own weight, but he was getting weaker.

Wade was putting more pressure on his bad leg than he should have, but there was no way Randi could hold any more of his massive bulk. She wasn't sure how much more she could endure. As much as you have to, she chastised herself, *as much as you have to.*

The bright moon lit the way and they traveled in silence—each lost in their own thoughts. Besides, it took too much effort to talk. She'd told Wade if he could do this, then so could she, but she was beginning to have her doubts. Running through the woods at night was one thing. Lugging around a grown man was something else altogether.

She shifted the position of his arm, trying to ease the spot rubbing her shoulder. *Put one foot in front of the other. Think about something besides what's behind us.* She needed a distraction from her sore feet and aching back. But she also needed to stop, to rest—if only for a few moments.

Without speaking, Wade tugged on her and veered off to the right, stopping at a fallen tree. Grateful beyond words, Randi helped lower him to the log before dropping beside him. Breathing heavily, she braced her arms on her legs and hung her head.

"Thought we both needed a break." His own breath

was none too even.

She let out a snort. "Wh-whatever gave you that idea?" she managed. Her chest still heaved from the exertion and all she wanted to do was lie down and sleep for a couple of days. As tired as she was, though, she couldn't keep her mind from wandering. Did Wade's coming for her mean he'd forgiven her? Had he decided to not disrupt their daughter's life? Or was he merely doing his job as an FBI agent? She wished she knew. At least he didn't seem as upset with her as he'd been when he'd stormed off this morning.

A moment passed before he laid a hand on her arm. She finally looked at him and almost drowned in the tenderness and compassion she saw in his eyes. And the pain. She shoved her thoughts to the back of her mind to focus on the here and now. "Sorry. How's the leg?" She nodded toward his injury.

"It'll do," he replied without taking his gaze off her face.

Randi swallowed—hard—at the look he was sending her. She swore he was going to kiss her. This didn't seem the time or the place, but darned if she didn't want him to do exactly that. With every fiber in her being, she wanted nothing more than to be held by him, to have his fingers curled in her hair and his warm lips pressed to hers.

His eyelids drooped as he leaned toward her. Heart pounding against her chest, she touched the tip of her tongue to her lips to moisten them. Her breath caught in her throat in anticipation. She forgot all else—the abduction, the explosion, everything. Right here, right now, it was just the two of them. She leaned into him.

And he passed out.

Randi scrambled to catch him and maneuver him to the ground. She instantly thought of sheltering the injured leg, to keep from hurting it further while she managed to keep him from crumpling like a pretzel at her feet. "Wade? Wade!" she cried as she patted his cheek. Alarmed at his ashen appearance, she worried what to do.

Taking a deep breath, she struggled to calm herself. "Don't go getting hysterical. That won't help you any. And it sure won't help him." Two more deep breaths and her heart rate slowed.

The bright red on the bandage tied around his leg caught her eye and she forgot her terror. His wound was still bleeding. She scooted down the length of his body as her mind flashed on the power held within that frame, to the *weight* that frame carried. It was amazing to her they'd made it this far…that *she'd* made it this far. Shaking her head, she focused on his injury and not her own selfishness.

A second glance at his face told her he hadn't come to yet so she untied the blood-soaked handkerchief and methodically examined the wound. She needed a clean bandage.

And dry hands. She wiped as much of the blood off her hands as possible onto the lower leg of her pants, then yanked off her jacket.

She tugged and pulled at the sleeve of her top until it finally came loose. Slipping the cloth off her arm, she folded the cotton, made a good size square pad and pressed it against the gaping wound. She then used the soiled handkerchief to tie it securely in place. "A first aid kit and some antiseptic would be nice, but maybe this will help," she muttered.

She studied his profile; his hair rumpled, ash and dirt clinging to his face. He was beautiful if you could say that about a man. Unable to keep her hands off him, she moved to the upper part of his body, lifted his head and cradled it on her lap as she leaned back against the log.

"You're still white as a sheet, but your breathing is steadier," she whispered as she slid her fingers lightly over his cheek, down the stubble on his jaw. Lifting his hand, she placed a kiss on the palm. "You should have said something, you big oaf. Why didn't we stop sooner?"

Randi was unprepared for the hand that reached up behind her neck and pulled her face down to his as the fingers on Wade's other hand gripped hers. Her lips met his and there was nothing but heat—and desperate need. She wasn't sure if he was fully awake. It didn't matter. She returned the kiss with equal fervor, more than willing to drown in the essence of him.

Heat pooled in the pit of her stomach as he ran his fingers through her hair. He teased her lips with his tongue and when she opened to him, slipped inside to spar with her tongue.

"I—I need…" he murmured against her as he twisted around, then drew her down next to him, frantically kissing her eyes, her lips, nibbling on her neck. "Beautiful—dream."

She stilled and drew back. *Dream?* Opening her eyes, she studied him. His eyes were still shut and he fumbled at the front of her blouse, cupping her. For another moment she basked at his touch and the sensations it sent through her. Loving the way her body automatically arched against him. Loving the way he made her want him inside her. Reluctantly, she shoved away from him.

"Mmph, no. Don't go."

Tears stung her eyes. She wanted him to make love to her, but not like this. Not here. "Wade. Wade! Wake up." At first, she shook him gently. Then harder.

His hands stilled a moment before they dropped away from her. His eyelids fluttered, then slowly opened. He looked confused, but smoky desire still lingered in his eyes. A look she knew was reflected in her own eyes. "Hey."

"Ah, what happened?"

"You passed out."

Shock registered on his face as he struggled to sit up and looked around. "How long? How long have I been out?" Urgency tinted his voice.

"Not long. Maybe five minutes." It had been a little longer, but she didn't want to tell him. "You pushed yourself too hard. You've lost a lot of blood."

Gingerly, he ran a hand over the new bandage. "You've been busy, I see." A corner of his lips twitched upward.

"Ah, shucks, dude. T'wernt nothin'," she replied in a mock southern drawl. "Don't reckon I needed that sleeve, anyhow. By the way, it looks like something hit you at an angle and took a chunk out of your calf. You've got a jagged gash but it doesn't look like there are any foreign objects left in your leg."

He nodded, then grimaced. "Thank you. After what I said this morning, I'm surprised you didn't leave me for dead. I wouldn't have blamed you if you had."

She studied him a long moment, then said quietly, "I'd never do that."

He opened his mouth to say something, closed it, ran a hand through his already tousled hair, then turned his head away from her. Pulling himself up on the log, he gently put a little pressure on the injured leg.

Deflated, but determined to not be defeated, Randi pressed on. "What were you going to say, Wade? Despite what you may think of me, I'm not the heartless shrew you think I am. I really am a good person. Ask anyone who knows me. And if how you responded to my presence when you came to a few minutes ago is any indication, then—"

He jerked her to him, crushing his mouth against hers. Shocked, she didn't respond at first, but when he wrapped his arms around her, she melted. She slid her arms around his neck, but he pulled away.

"Now look here, Wade Ma—"

"Hush. Listen." He held his fingers to her lips.

That's when she heard the voice. Faint, but distinctive.

"Do you hear me, Malone? I'm coming for you! I'll catch you. Then you get to watch me kill your girlfriend, right before I kill you. Do you hear me, Malone? You're a dead man!"

Then the laughter Randi recognized so well rang out. The hysterical, crazy laughter of the kidnapper.

Wade checked his phone again, then cursed. Still no cell service. They were on their own. He replaced it, then grabbed her jacket and tossed it to her as he staggered to his feet. She shoved her arms in the sleeves and moved to his side to serve as a crutch, ready to put some distance between them and the kidnapper.

"Wait," he said as his hand went to his holster, then began searching the ground. "Where is it? Did you see

142

it?"

"See what?"

"My gun. It had to have fallen out of the holster when I blacked out. Help me find it."

Dropping to her knees, she searched the area around them. Checking behind the log, she didn't find it there, either. "Are you sure it would have dropped out here? I don't remember seeing it. In fact, I don't remember feeling it against me after we left the barn."

He stopped, a strange look on his face, then he cursed. "I must have dropped it during the blast. I had it in my hand right before I saw you."

Panic inched its way up her spine. This night just kept getting worse. "Oh, no. What are we going to do? You don't happen to have any other weapons on you, do you?"

He shook his head. "We have to find better cover, then we'll worry about weapons. Okay?" He touched her arm briefly while he studied the terrain with a trained eye.

As he draped his arm over her shoulders, Randi recognized that steely look in his eyes, the determined set of his jaw. Given their circumstances, and his weakened state, she hoped his stubbornness and cunning would be enough.

It had to be.

Chapter Ten

Wade cursed his injured leg. He set his jaw, irritation flooding him. If he hadn't been injured, they'd be making better time. In fact, he could've made sure Miranda was safe, then gone after the kidnapper and left her totally out of it. But he *was* hurt. Every painful step he took was a constant reminder.

He gritted his teeth as wave after wave of pain shot up his leg each time he put pressure on it. Miranda was doing her best, but she was having a hard time holding him up. To give her credit, she hadn't whined or complained, even though she must be exhausted. Hell, he wasn't in too good a shape himself.

How far had they come? The thick foliage made it difficult to tell. "Wait," he whispered to her, and she came to a staggering halt. Even with the cool evening air, sweat beaded on her brow and glistened in the moonlight. She didn't look at him, but leaned into him. She continued to breathe heavily. Sheer determination must be the only thing keeping her going, he mused.

"I wish we could rest a bit, but I don't think we should chance it."

She glanced at him with regret in her eyes, then nodded in understanding.

He tucked a wayward strand of hair behind her ear and caressed her cheek. As he planted a kiss on her forehead, he glanced behind them. The glow of the burning barn behind them lit the night sky. The similarities between this, and his experiences in the jungles of South America were uncanny. But this wasn't Columbia, this was Arkansas. He sucked in a shuddering breath to refocus. Time was of an essence and he had to keep his thoughts in the present in order to get them both out of this alive.

"Hey, Malone! Do you hear me? I'm com-i-n-g for you."

Then that awful laughter…the maniacal cackling of an insane person.

She whimpered and slipped from his grasp as her knees hit the ground. "No. I can't do this anymore. It's too much, Wade. Too much."

Afraid to bend down too far and not be able to get back up himself, he grabbed her upper arm and yanked, forcing her back on her feet. Then he shook her. "Listen to me. Listen! I need you to stay with me."

Trying to pull from his grasp, she shook her head as tears streamed down her face, her eyes wide with fear. "No," she said weakly.

He took control and forced her to face him, turning her away from the glowing skyline. "Yes. We can beat this. We can beat him, Miranda," he said more gently. He placed a hand on the back of her neck and pulled her to him, then kissed her. Hard. At first, she kept fighting him, then relaxing, she kissed him back. When she slid her arms around his neck, he knew he had won. He softened the kiss before pulling away.

She slumped against him and hiccupped. "Did you mean it? What you just said?"

"We *can* beat him, babe. We're smarter than him.

But we'll have to do it together. Do you trust me?" He held his breath. If she fell apart on them, with his injury, they'd never make it.

"Yes, I've always trusted you."

He raised an eyebrow and wanted desperately to ask her more. But now wasn't the time.

"A—all right then. What do we do?" she asked.

"You're the one familiar with this area. Which way do we go?"

She looked around; confusion etched on her face. "I—I don't know. I'm all turned around. The barn is behind us so the house is farther back from that. If we circle around, I suppose we'd eventually come to the highway, but I've never been out here at night."

Miranda took a few steps away as Wade leaned against a tree. She slowly turned around in a circle, with her eyes closed. *What is she doing?* She stopped, then pointed to the right. He had expected her to go left, as that appeared to be the best, and easiest, route back to the house.

"This way. We have to go this way," she said emphatically.

He gestured toward the left. "But I thought—"

"Nope. This way."

He wondered if she was the one losing her mind, not the lunatic behind them. At least she wasn't hysterical. But the transformation was so sudden he had serious doubts about her.

"I'm all right now. I know where we have to go." A gentle smile played on her lips. "I told you I trusted you. Now I need you to trust me."

Skeptical, but willing to give whatever plan she had a shot, he merely nodded. "You can tell me on the way. I think we'd better get moving." The sound of the kidnapper thrashing through the woods echoed closer.

****

Randi didn't know how or why; she just knew they had to veer off to the right. Maybe it was adrenaline, or maybe she was beyond exhaustion, but she didn't feel the pain of holding Wade up anymore. Tree limbs continued to slap her in the face, brambles pulled and tugged at her slacks and sweat ran down between her breasts. But for the first time in hours, she had real hope.

"Want to tell me where we're going?"

"I don't know. Exactly." She thought about not telling him the truth, but decided honesty was the best policy. Look where keeping secrets from him had gotten her.

"Well, figure it out *exactly* because it sure looks like we're headed deeper into the woods—not closer to civilization," he growled.

She'd overlook his short temper because of his injury. But later, after they were safe, she was definitely going to have a serious talk with him about attitudes.

"You said you'd trust me. I don't know how—I just know it will be all right." She felt his muscles tense through the fabric of her jacket and envisioned steam coming out of his ears, but he kept moving. And he didn't question her further.

She was grateful for small favors, but where was she taking them? *Trust your instincts...trust yourself.*

They kept walking, stumbling mostly, for what felt like hours. It hadn't been that long, though, because light from the fire still burned behind them, even though it was beginning to fade. And eerily the kidnapper was still on their trail, making no effort to be quiet.

How much longer can Wade—no, we—keep going? He wasn't the only one losing his battle with fatigue. The adrenaline rush was definitely over.

He tripped over a rock and fell to his knees, pulling her down with him as he ground out a curse. "Miranda, you've got to go get help." Defeat rang in his voice.

She blew out a deep breath in an attempt to get her pounding heart under control. "No. I—I told you before, I won't leave you. How—how in the world do you think you can fight him off? With your charm and good looks? I don't think so." Making light of the situation was the only way for her to deal with the possibility they both might die. And fairly soon if she didn't get them to where they had to be…wherever that was.

He glared at her, but soon his lips twitched and a rumble began in his chest. Dropping back onto the ground, he stretched his leg out then laughed. Loud.

"Shh. What are you trying to do, tell him exactly where we are?" She was appalled he was giving their position away.

"Hey, Ma-lo-ne! Having fun? Enjoy it while you can cause you ain't going to be around much longer."

"Ah, darling, he knows where we are. In fact, he's probably got night vision goggles and is watching us right now. He's been toying with us like your cat with a mouse."

All the energy drained out of her. "So, we just sit here and wait for him? Is that your plan?"

"Well, for the moment, more or less. This is your fault, you know."

"Mine?"

"Yeah, I'm so sweet and lovable I'll just *charm* him into total submission when he shows up."

Admittedly she did say that. But to totally give them away? "Wade, get a grip," she demanded as she shook him.

Then the steely look was back. All laughter vanished as quickly as it had materialized. "Now that I've got you mad again, can we go?"

"You did that on purpose." She punched him lightly in the arm.

"Ow. Watch it."

"You're a jerk, you know that?"

"No, actually, I'm a sorry SOB. I messed up and allowed that lunatic to take you in the first place. I should have anticipated this." He struggled to get the words out as she helped him to his feet.

Now *that* made her stop. "It's not your fault. There's no way you even knew he was stalking you," she whispered, tears pooling in her eyes.

"Right now, it doesn't matter. Got your breath back?"

"I'm better. How are you holding up?" She swiped a hand across her face. She wasn't the one who'd lost blood or walked who-knew-how-far on an injured leg.

"I always get the job done. One way or the other, and this will be no exception."

Stubborn to the core, she knew he meant it. Smiling to herself, she draped his arm over her shoulder. "We need to angle more to the left from here on."

"I thought you said you didn't know where we were," he accused.

"Um, I do but I don't."

"What does that mean?"

"I'm not sure. But while we were taking our break back there, it finally dawned on me what I'd been trying to remember." Yes, this definitely felt right. She didn't want to jinx anything by talking about it too soon, though.

He gripped her shoulder a little harder to get her full attention. "What are you getting at?"

"Not yet. Just a little farther." As it turned out, it took longer to get there than she thought. They came to an exceptionally thick area of foliage, and Wade pulled them to the right.

"No, this way," she insisted as she struggled to go straight ahead.

"I'm sorry, babe, but I don't have the strength to go any farther, and I sure don't feel like fighting my way through there." He nodded in the direction she was so determined to go.

"Please, Wade. This is where you have to trust me. And make one last effort. Come on, you can do it," she encouraged.

He had gotten so weak she practically pulled him through the vines and limbs blocking their way, batting them out of his face the best she could.

And into a clearing.

****

Phillip chuckled. Malone was getting weaker. They were moving slower, so in turn, he'd slowed his own pace. *This is fun!* Teasing and tormenting them was more satisfying than he'd thought it would be. Of course, the fed didn't have a weapon, so all the man could do was tuck his tail and hide like a dog.

"Keep running, Malone! I know you won't stand up and fight me," he yelled. No, the fed had begun his career by shooting his kid brother in the back. What kind of man did that? The cop didn't deserve compassion or consideration.

And today he was going to get what was coming to him. *Your death is going to be painful. I hope you haven't lost too much blood, because I don't want you passing out on me before I'm finished with you...or your girlfriend.*

Suddenly tired of the game, he picked up his pace.

Time to end it. Here. Now.

****

Wade staggered to a stop as they broke through the barrier of deep foliage and came into a clearing...with no coverage from the person pursuing them.

"Why did you bring us this direction? We don't have time, or the energy, to move to a better location." He failed miserably at keeping the irritation—and defeat—out of his voice.

"I was following my instincts, Wade."

He blew out an unsteady breath. "Well, it isn't enough. There isn't time for us to get across the field before he catches us."

"We don't need to get across the field. And I'm willing to bet my life on my instinct." She glared at him in defiance.

"Well, I'm not." He turned and began following the tree line, looking for anything to use as a weapon, preferably something hard. "Doesn't this infernal mountain have any rocks I can use on it?"

She didn't answer him, and he was grateful. Her posture and the stubborn expression on her face told him she thought everything was fine simply because they'd come to that clearing. If only that were true. It was time for a showdown while he still had some strength left, and he needed something to fight with.

"What can I do to help?"

"So, you admit you might be wrong?"

"No. I'm not saying that at all. What I'm saying—"

A gunshot cut through the air and echoed through the woods. It wasn't too close, but close enough. Automatically, he wrapped his arms around her and shoved her to the ground. The sudden movement sent another sharp pain up his leg. "Dammit! That's what I was afraid of," he ground out through clenched teeth.

"Maybe that's the sheriff trying to let us know he's there. Won't they come investigate the explosion and fire?" Hope reflected in her tone as they slowly struggled back to their feet.

"Don't kid yourself, it's not Bennett. Even if he's at the barn, he won't know to come looking for us here." He searched the ground for a sturdy limb. Finally, he found what he'd been looking for. "Get that for me, will you? It's not my weapon of choice, but it'll have to do."

She let go of him, and he had to hobble on his good leg to maintain his balance. He had a sinking feeling that after all these years, his luck had run out. Why had he been allowed to survive the tortures in South America, face death numerous times in his job with the Bureau then finally find Miranda again, only to have his life end here?

His strength ebbed with each beat of his heart. Surely, Miranda realized it too. She was the one who had been holding him up. And now the madman was the only one armed.

They didn't stand a chance.

"Help me over to that large tree, then keep going. Stay out of the clearing. Circle back to your place and call the sheriff."

"I'm not leaving you," she said adamantly.

"You're so cute when you're being stubborn." On impulse, and because he knew he'd never see her again, he leaned down and pressed his lips to hers. His senses were assaulted by her taste—her beautifully responsive lips and the pressure of her soft breasts against his chest as she leaned into him. He'd carry the memories with him for the rest of his life, which wouldn't be that much longer if the gunman had his way.

Before Wade allowed himself the luxury of drowning in Miranda's kiss, he pulled back. He had to get her away from here while there was still time. However, her whimper almost undid him. Steeling himself, he set her away. "Give me the limb."

She glanced down at the piece of wood in her hand, as if she'd forgotten it was there. Without a word, she handed it over. He placed his other hand on her shoulder, and using her as a crutch again, limped over to the tree.

Once there, he placed his back against it for support. "Now, go on. Get out of here." He tried to keep the desperation out of his voice, but failed.

"No."

"Woman—"

"I can't leave you here like this. You can't beat him by yourself, you're too weak."

She was right, but that was beside the point. There was no way he'd put her life in anymore danger than it

153

had been already. He'd find the strength. After all, he'd managed to get out of the jungle. Surely, he'd find a way out of these woods.

Alive.

Indecision was evident in her tone and from her expression. As he watched, she swayed in her decision, then he saw the resignation in her eyes.

"I need to know you're okay," he implored her.

She gently stroked his cheek, gave him a quick kiss, then laid her forehead against his. "I've always loved you," she whispered before she turned away and ran down the tree line a short distance. Then she was gone as she dodged back into the thick foliage.

Wade had never felt so alone, even in the jungle. Regret flooded him. If he got out of this... But the likelihood of that happening was slim to none. All the cards were stacked against him.

For the first time, he truly understood what it was like to be hunted, to be on the other end. *Well, now I know.* He'd never look at another perpetrator the same way again. A snort escaped his lips. *What's the matter with me? I don't have a snowballs chance of surviving.*

He thought about glancing around the tree to see how close the kidnapper was, but decided against it. If his assumption was right, and the madman *did* have night vision goggles, then he'd be spotted, blowing his element of surprise. However, up to this point, the man hadn't made any effort to be quiet.

Oh, hell! That's what's missing...noise. He's sneaking up on me. Bitterly, he cursed himself for being distracted and not paying closer attention to their purser. Every muscle in his body tensed and adrenaline pulsed through him. With all his might, he hoped

Miranda had gotten far enough away from the area that she'd reach safety. A slight movement caught his attention. With the tree limb gripped firmly in his hands, he waited.

With a stealth the man hadn't shown so far, he came into view...a gun in his hand. He stopped, just out of reach, surveying the area. Thoughts flashed through Wade's mind as he flattened himself against the tree...a tree that didn't seem nearly big enough now.

The man finally took a couple steps closer. Gathering his flagging strength, Wade gripped the branch with both hands, and hoped the skills he had learned over the years would be enough.

He swung the limb and made good connection as he struck the man across the chest. The perpetrator grunted under the impact and staggered back, but he didn't fall and he didn't release the gun. Wade pulled back to strike again, but the pursuer ducked the blow. On the third attempt to use the limb as a club, the other man grabbed it and the two men became engaged in a tug-of-war. The man held on with only one hand, where Wade had to use both of his. And for the first time, Wade got a good look at the man who so desperately wanted him dead.

Wade blinked. The man from the café. The one who had talked to Miranda at the gas station. For a fraction of a second, he wondered if she was in cahoots with him, then immediately dismissed the idea. She had proven herself a hundred-fold since the barn had blown up. The man was good at putting down smoke screens. *But who-in-the-hell-was he?* And why did he want Wade dead? Another sharp tug on the limb dispelled any other thoughts as he fought for his life.

Yanking, tugging, and shoving, they struggled for the piece of wood. Wade managed to keep him off balance enough so he couldn't use the gun he gripped in his other hand. But Wade was tiring quickly. He would die…just like the man said. He only hoped Miranda had had enough time to get help. Even if the guy killed him, Wade wanted the man caught and prosecuted.

The bark of the wood bit into his skin, and he was having a hard time staying on his feet. Waiting until the perpetrator leaned backwards, Wade let go. The man landed with a thud. Ignoring his injured leg, Wade jumped on him, struggling to reach the gun. If he could gain control of it, he might have a surviving chance.

Then the weapon discharged.

Both men froze. Wade was the first to realize neither of them had been hit and punched him in the face. But the blows were too soft. His strength was fading rapidly. Then he was thrown onto his back as the other man rolled to his feet.

Wade made a grab for him, but missed as the perpetrator backed up a few steps, wiped the blood from his mouth and pointed the gun at him. *This is it.*

The man laughed as Wade pushed himself to a sitting position. "Look at this. The mighty Malone, special agent for the FBI, beaten and sittin' in the dirt. And I'm the one who did it!" he crowed.

Wade drew his eyebrows together and glowered at him. No one had laughed at him in a long time. If he had any strength left, the other man would not only be sitting in the dirt right now, he'd be eating it. But with a gun pointed at his head and several feet between them, Wade had few options. But first, he wanted some answers.

"How'd you do it?"

The gunman looked confused for a moment, then his cocky attitude came back. "Do what? Beat you? Easy, man."

Wade resisted a snarky comeback about how he had to be injured for the man to get the upper hand. "No, how'd you track us? I figured you had night vision goggles, but I don't see any."

He snorted. "I didn't need anything like that. I was born and raised in the backwoods and can track anything or anybody, day or night. Besides, you made enough noise that it was easy to follow you. I just hung back to see how far you'd get."

Just as Wade suspected. The man had waited for Wade to weaken before trying to overtake him. Unfortunately, he had succeeded.

"Say, where's your little whore?" he asked as he studied the woods. "You don't want to miss out on the fun I've got planned for her, now do you?"

Wade's blood ran cold. More than ever, he hoped she'd make it back to her place and call Bennett. If she wasn't safe, then all his efforts were for nothing. "Gone," he said in a flat tone.

"Oh, really? I doubt she left you so easily."

"I sent her for the sheriff a while back. They'll be arriving soon." *Please keep going, Miranda.*

"Why do I have a hard time believing that? But it's too bad she's not here. We all could've had some fun. Maybe I'll catch up with her later," he said with a sneer.

Wade noticed their surroundings. During their struggle, they had wound up away from the trees, and the gunman stood in the open meadow. Why had

Miranda been so insistent they come there? What was so special about this field? There was no cover, nothing to use as a weapon. But, at this point, it didn't matter. "Before you kill me—"

"So, you finally realize I'm going to be the one to give you what you deserve? I'm sure there are a lot of people out there who will want to throw a parade in my honor for getting rid of you."

"Yeah, I'll bet," Wade said dryly.

"You're a legend. Everyone wants you dead."

"How flattering. Too bad I don't give a damn about any of the slime balls you associate with."

"Watch it," he growled, pointing the gun in a menacing manner.

"Touch a nerve, slug breath?" Perversely, he couldn't help but taunt the man. Wade struggled to gain his footing. If he was going to die, he wanted to be standing on his own two feet, not cowering in the dirt. "Tell me, what exactly was it I did to you to be *honored* with your obsessive desire to put a bullet between my eyes?"

"Oh, don't worry. Your death won't be nearly that quick." The man paced a few feet away, his fingers flexing repeatedly around the grip of the gun as he walked.

"And you hate me because...?"

"Does the name Patrick Fry mean anything to you?"

The name sounded vaguely familiar, but he couldn't quite place it. "Naw. Sounds like any other scumbag's name to me."

He cocked the gun. "You don't even remember. Figures. The man was responsible for your rapid rise with the Feds and you dismiss him as if he were a piece of garbage."

Wade was smart enough to keep his mouth shut, so he waited.

"Your first case. In North Dakota." The gun barrel drooped as the man relaxed his grip.

Then Wade remembered. "Oh, yeah, the cop killer. So, what was he to you?"

"My brother," he hissed.

That explained a lot. "So that makes you...?"

"Phillip Fry"

The name didn't ring a bell, but if he was anything like his brother, he was sneaky as hell and just as deadly.

"You killed him in cold blood. He didn't have a chance." Fry's face was mottled with rage.

Wade started to lunge at him, but stopped when the gun pointed toward his heart again. "Oh, he had a chance, all right. Which is more than he gave his victims.

"He had multiple opportunities to give himself up during the stand-off. Instead, he shot one agent in the back and had a bead on another. I had no choice but to take him down. The man he killed has a little boy who's growing up without his father. I don't know what you call it where you come from, but from where I stand, *that's* injustice."

"You don't know anything, Malone...about me or my family. But I know all about you."

"What do you mean?"

"Hell, I've been tracking your career since the day I found out you were the one to take out Patrick. I know everything there is to know," Fry boasted. "Didn't know about your little girlfriend here until the other day, though. You sure managed to keep her under wraps. But I have to admit, she came in useful in getting you lured out here. I'll give her a special thank you a little later."

Wade narrowed his eyes. "Why not forget her? She doesn't have anything to do with this." It was useless to ask, but he did anyway.

"Tsk, tsk, Malone. I never leave unfinished business. I'll tend to her shortly." He paused as the wild gleam of his eyes reflected in the moonlight. "Times up."

Wade stiffened, not quite ready to give up, but not sure how to prevent the man from putting a bullet in his heart. Fry had a feverish look on his face, and began pointing the gun at different parts of Wade's body. No, his heart would be the last place he got a bullet.

"Now, where shall we begin, hum?"

Chapter Eleven

Afraid to move any closer for fear she'd be heard by one of the men, Randi hid partly behind a small tree. They hadn't noticed her approach during their struggle, but now they stood talking.

The man, Phillip Fry she'd learned, implied things that chilled her to the bone. From her earlier exposure to him, she knew he was capable of anything.

If things went wrong, if Wade died, and Fry captured her again, she'd suffer a much worse outcome from when she had been his captive earlier. A shudder shook her. *It'll be all right. It'll work out. Have faith.* But Wade looked as if he were about to collapse. There was no fight left in him. She was surprised he had lasted this long.

Then Fry started waving the gun around, as if deciding which part of Wade's body to shoot first. Panic gripped her. She couldn't let this happen! She refused to lose Wade again, not like this. Then she remembered the baseball size rock she'd picked up and clutched to her chest. Was she close enough to hit Fry and do any good? It had been a long time since she'd played with the town's intermural softball team. She sucked at running, but had been able to throw home from left field. She prayed she hadn't lost her touch.

"Time to get this party started." Fry said with a

sneer as he cocked the hammer.

Before she could move, the scream of what sounded like a large cat echoed through the clearing. A cougar, or bobcat? Both men turned and Fry swung the gun in the direction of the sound. Cat or no cat, this was her chance. Adrenaline pumped through her. She said a quick prayer, then threw the rock with all she had left in her, striking him in the arm. He dropped the gun as he staggered. Wade picked up the discarded limb and struck him in the chest, knocking him farther backwards into the clearing.

There was a cracking sound. Fry screamed, then dropped out of sight. A moment later, she heard a loud thump. Randi had never been so glad for rotted wooden well coverings in her life.

Wade let go of the limb as he collapsed. Randi rushed to his side; the villain totally dismissed from her mind. They weren't in danger from him any longer. But Wade was still in grave need of medical attention. She stroked his cheek and found it clammy, his skin appeared ashen in the moonlight. "Oh, darling," she whispered as she lightly pressed her lips to his forehead.

His eyes opened to a tiny slit and he attempted a smile. It came out more of a grimace. "Wh-why didn't you keep going? I tol—told you to—"

"You fool. You didn't think I'd let you have all the fun now, did you?"

His eyes drifted shut.

"Do me a favor, will you, Malone?"

At the sound of his last name, he opened his eyes again. "Yeah?" his voice little more than a whisper.

"Don't go dying on me, will you? I need you."

This time he did smile. "I'll try my best," he managed to get out.

She tugged off her jacket and tucked it around him for warmth. "I'm going for help. Just you remember I'll be back. Okay?"

This time, he didn't respond. *Hurry,* was all she could think of. With one backward glance, she took off running, the urgency of the situation screaming at her. Half-way to the tree line she remembered his cell phone. Stopping dead in her tracks, she whirled around and rushed back to his side, only to find Sebastian perched next to him. Her cat had emitted that shrill cry? Who knew the cat had it in him? She didn't care. It had distracted Fry enough for she and Wade to take him down.

Still unconscious, the sight of Wade lying there, so vulnerable, practically brought her to her knees. This was the tough FBI agent who didn't give an inch. His sense of duty and determination to get justice was so great you couldn't help but appreciate it. She might not have known that a few days ago, but she knew it now.

She pulled the phone out of his jacket pocket and checked. She had reception! Dialing 9-1-1, she told the dispatcher what had happened, asking for medical assistance and also for the sheriff. She'd finally realized they were on the old Miller place, which had access from the road. Good. Going back through the woods to her house was farther than she wanted to go. Her body had reached its limit. Besides, she didn't want to leave Wade...or Sebastian.

Finally, after what felt like an eternity, but was more like fifteen minutes, the entire area was ablaze with flashing lights and people. Reminiscent of the crash scene, she was grateful there was only one fatality…and that it wasn't Wade.

Yet.

****

Randi chewed on a fingernail while holding on to her cat. The thought of Wade not surviving was unacceptable. "Do you think he'll be all right?"

Fatigue lined Sheriff Bennett's face. He glanced in the direction of the paramedics, "He lost a lot of blood," he said, a pained expression on his face.

"I know. He kept pushing himself, even though he was bleeding badly."

"But I'm not a doctor," he added, doubt tinging his voice.

She turned her head, unable to look the sheriff in the eye. *Please, God, let Wade live. Don't let me loose him a second time.* To take her mind off the only man she'd ever love, she asked, "Did you find him?"

"Who?"

"The man who tried to kill us. He's in the old well."

"Well?" He glanced in the direction of the hole everyone avoided. "We've been searching the area thinking the kidnapper was on the run, but never thought to look there. Wait here."

"Like I'm going to get up and run a marathon," she muttered to his retreating back. She was so tired she could sleep for a week and not wake up.

He yelled at some of the other men to bring a light and they clustered around the gaping hole. One man lay on his stomach and scooted over to the opening, with another holding onto his legs to keep him from accidentally falling in. "There's someone down there all right," she heard him say, followed by, "Looks like we can call off the manhunt." Then Jake and two men in suits came back to her.

"Randi Johnson, this is Special Agent Smith and Special Agent Wesson from the Federal Bureau of Investigation. They'd like to get your statement."

She started to giggle, then stopped herself. Exhaustion was playing havoc with her emotions, but dang, the agents names tickled her funny bone. "Wish I'd had you a while ago," she said, thinking of a Smith and Wesson handgun, and not one of the men. Although, they could have come in handy, too.

"I'm sorry we weren't able to aid you previously, Ms. Johnson," Agent Smith said, apparently unaware of her meaning. Or so used to the comments he ignored them.

"Randi?" Jake asked. "Can you tell us what happened?"

She liked that he'd used her first name. If his intention was to put her at ease, he succeeded. She hesitated. Where should she begin?

"We'd like to understand what this was all about. Agent Malone isn't in any shape to provide information surrounding your kidnapping and the subsequent events, so your cooperation is appreciated," Agent Wesson said.

"So, what do you want to know?" She was too tired to think.

It was Agent Smith who spoke this time. "Do you know who the man is that tried to kill you?"

Wow, they do that tag team thing really well. "Oh, um, yeah, he did say his name. It was—something Fry, I think."

Agent Smith pulled out his phone and tapped on the screen a minute. He finally looked up. "Phillip Fry. It appears Agent Malone was responsible for his brother's death a few years ago."

"He did mention his brother. But I wasn't close enough to hear his name, though. Why did Wade shoot the brother?" She paused and waved her hand in the air. "Never mind. I don't think I want to know."

The agent stepped toward her and leveled a stare at her. "You should know if he hadn't acted when he did, a fellow agent would have died. Malone was doing the job he was trained to do."

Wow. She gave a small nod.

"He's a good agent…a good man. One of our finest," Agent Wesson added.

"Thank you for telling me." Then she quickly filled them in on the events of the evening, leaving out how close she and Wade had become, and all the while she kept her gaze on the man who held her heart. Finally satisfied, both men thanked her, then shook hands with Sheriff Bennett and walked over to the pit.

The paramedics lifted the stretcher with Wade on it and carried it to the helicopter that had landed only minutes ago. "Can I…?" She wanted to climb in there with him.

The sheriff shook his head. "No. But I'll make sure you get to the hospital. You need to be checked out, too."

She waved him off. "I'm fine."

"Why are the women in this town so hardheaded?" he muttered to himself.

Randi wanted to tell him they had to be to survive, especially when the men they depended on wouldn't, or couldn't, stick around. At the moment, though, she didn't have the strength to set him straight.

"I need to make sure you're all right." He sounded tired. She wasn't the only one who'd had a rough day. Turning to his deputy, he said, "Take care of her."

"Yes, sir." Clay took her elbow. "Can you walk? Or do I need to carry you? It'd be my pleasure, you know." He wiggled his eyebrows, then winked.

"So you and Roy would have something to rib me about next time we go for a ride? I don't think so." Bless his heart. He'd lightened the mood and it gave her enough energy to put one foot in front of the other as they headed toward one of the SUV's sitting in the clearing. "Will you make sure Sebastian gets back to the house? I think all these people are scaring him."

Clay raised his eyebrows, as if he didn't believe her. Cradled in her arms, the cat purred his contentment.

The blades from the helicopter sped up and she covered her face, and Sebastian's, from flying debris as the helicopter took off, carrying the only man she'd ever loved. She prayed he survived. If she lost him this time, she wasn't sure *she'd* survive.

****

Wade awoke to bright lights and the smell of antiseptic. *I hate hospitals.* He was hooked up to a machine and had an IV in his arm, probably a blood transfusion. Then he glanced to his right. Miranda was curled up in the large visitor chair, asleep.

Despite the dark circles under her eyes, she still looked peaceful and beautiful. The debris had been combed out of her hair, she'd washed the dirt and blood off, and had even changed clothes.

The door to his room swished open, and a nurse came in. She narrowed her gaze at the sleeping woman, then looked at him. "No visitors allowed," she said as she moved to the chair, apparently intent on removing the unwanted woman.

"Leave her," he growled.

The nurse hesitated. "Sir, if she isn't family, she can't stay here."

Miranda wasn't going to leave his side if she didn't want to. Wade didn't care who told him otherwise, she was staying. The older nurse glared down at him as if she were a Marine Corps drill sergeant. He was sure that look had stopped a lot of people in their tracks.

He wasn't fazed.

"Woman, if you wake her up, I'm going to rip this needle out of my arm and ram it up your ass," he said with barely controlled anger.

She must have believed him because she backed away before she scurried out the door, quietly closing it behind her. Miranda didn't stir a muscle.

Wade dropped his head back onto the pillow, mentally replaying the evenings events. Until he'd seen that message on the motel mirror, he thought he hated her, was totally over her. She didn't have a place in his life, hadn't for years. He'd been fine with that. Had learned to live without her, had shoved all emotions into a steel vault and done an exemplary job for the bureau. Now, after everything that had happened tonight, all of his emotions flooded back. Watching her sleep made him long for things that could never be, for the life they'd originally planned.

Tonight, was an example of what he dealt with on a regular basis. They had both come close to being killed simply because of who he was, what he did for a living. He was nothing but bad news for her—a beacon to all the creeps he'd dealt with over the years to track him down. He'd made so many enemies that if he stayed, she'd never be safe. He refused to subject her to that life.

He suppressed a deep sigh and fought the sting of unexpected tears. The gut-wrenching decision rivalled the heartache of when he'd returned from the jungle only to find her gone. He hated what he was about to do to her, but for her own good, for her own safety, he had to move on. Alone. That meant leaving his daughter behind, too.

Miranda was right. Their child was better off with the people currently raising her. It was the safest thing for her. His heart gave another hard thump. Damn, but he wanted to get to know her. Not happening, though. Perhaps Miranda would tell him where she was so he could watch from afar. A new ache, a different kind of ache, settled over him. The old saying about losing a piece of yourself when someone you knew died was true. Even though she was still alive, a huge piece of Wade would remain in Arkansas, literally, and he'd never even met her. Didn't have to. He knew she was here, somewhere. Suppressing a groan, he doubled up in pain. How could he leave his child?

How could he leave Miranda?

That was exactly what he'd do, though. It ripped his heart out, but there was no other way. She deserved the kind of life he could never give her.

As if she felt his intense gaze, her eyes fluttered open and a slow smile spread across her lips. "Hey. You're awake."

Her voice floated across his skin, touching his soul. *Push her away. Don't let her care anymore than she already does. You're leaving, remember?* Instead, he heard himself say, "You're so beautiful."

Automatically her hand went to her hair and smoothed it back, a deep blush coloring her cheeks. The woman had no concept of the effect she had on him.

"You're an amazing man, you know that Agent Malone?"

With deliberate movements, she uncurled her legs and stood, holding on to the chair a moment to steady herself, then moved to him, sitting on the side of the bed. She slowly leaned down until she was within a fraction of an inch from his lips. A radiant smile lit up her face.

Oh, she knew what she was doing all right, he thought, the little vixen. And she knew his reaction to her. But he was determined to protect her. He couldn't let her get her hopes up, only to have them dashed. Even as he vowed to himself to push her away, he found his hand curling in her hair and pulling her lips to his. One last kiss. That's all he needed. If he could have one last taste, he could live the rest of his life alone.

He hoped.

Wonder and amazement exploded in him. She was so sweet, so sensuous, so unbelievably trusting. Unable to get enough of her, he deepened the kiss, exploring her mouth as she opened to him. He wanted her so bad it hurt. She moaned and twisted around to lay on the bed with him. It tore his heart out, but he had to stop.

Pulling back, he looked into her sea-green eyes, filled with desire. His heart in his throat, he couldn't talk about the passion, or his feelings right now, so he redirected her attention. "How long have you been in that chair?"

She gave him another quick peck before saying, "Not long. I've been waiting for you to come to."

Not quite knowing how to respond, he held up the arm with the IV. "I see they're feeding me."

"You were awfully weak. You lost a lot of blood and—and I was so worried." Tears filled her eyes, but didn't spill over. "The doctor said it'll take a while for the transfusion but you'll be okay. They stitched up your leg, by the way. You're going to have a scar."

"It's nothing. I've had worse." At the stricken look on her face, he wished he hadn't said the last part. She didn't need to know about his job or the dangers involved, at least not any more than she'd been exposed to already .

Sobering, he had to make her leave before he lost his nerve altogether. It took everything in him to push her away, to school his features into one of indifference. But he did for her sake. For his daughter's sake. "You can go home now."

"No. I want to stay until you go back to sleep. I—"

He hardened his tone. "I don't need you here."

Shock and surprise filled her face. "But…"

"Everything's over and you're safe. As soon as they release me, I'll head back to Kansas City."

Wide-eyed, her mouth opened and closed a couple times with no words coming out. This was killing him. "Look, I'm tired and need some rest." Faking a yawn, he turned away. He didn't want to see the hurt radiating off her. He closed his eyes and evened out his breathing —pretending to drift off to sleep. She sat there for a long while, probably watching him. There was nothing more he wanted than to throw his arms around her and hold her tight. But this was best for her. Finally, the bed moved as she stood, and moments later, the door swished closed.

He was such an ass.

Chapter Twelve

Randi couldn't believe what had happened. Wade had told her to leave, not just the room, but him. Why? After everything they had endured in the woods and survived, she was positive their love for each other had also survived. And that kiss. If that wasn't the kiss of someone who wanted her in his life, then what was it?

Her eyes stung with unshed tears and, as she passed the nurses station, the gray-haired nurse at first glared at her, then softened her features. The nurse wasn't totally heartless. Unwilling to meet anyone she might know in the elevator, Randi pushed open the door to the stairwell. It was cool and quiet and she breathed a sigh of relief. Peace. Which lasted less than thirty seconds when a door thumped closed somewhere above her.

Still holding the tears at bay, she hurried down the four flights of stairs to the main level. A small sitting area—partially obscured—sat off to the side and she ducked in there. Thankfully, no one else occupied the space. Hidden behind a large round column, she sank into a chair and sobbed. All the lost years, all the love they had shared... She'd thought that after Wade had come to her rescue, he had forgiven her. That he understood about the baby.

Didn't he understand a piece of her heart would

always be missing because she didn't have her daughter with her? Didn't he understand she was incomplete? Didn't he understand how lonely she was? She hid out in her house painting because she was unable to face the world on a daily basis. No one, not even Melody, knew her darkest secrets.

A tiny ray of sunshine had seeped into her world when Wade had walked back into her life a few days ago. For a brief time, she'd thought they would be able to patch things up...until he'd learned about the pregnancy. Then the little bit of love she'd seen in him died a scorching death.

Until he'd come to her rescue at the barn.

Then, she thought everything had changed.

Randi pulled a tissue out of her pocket and blew her nose, hoping no one would hear her and come to investigate. Folks from small-town America had a tendency to stick their noses where it wasn't needed or wanted, even though they had good intentions. When no one peered around the column, she relaxed.

She replayed the evening's events leading up to, and including Wade's actions a few minutes ago. But for the life of her, she couldn't make sense of it. All of her life, she'd felt alone. First her parent's divorce. Then her mom marrying a man so controlling Randi had quickly learned to become invisible, to be nothing more than bland wallpaper so no one noticed.

The only time she hadn't felt alone was in Wade's arms. Then, she'd been safe. She'd been loved. She'd felt like somebody and could conquer the world. If the success of her art business was any indication, she *had* conquered the world, albeit a small slice of it.

Drying her eyes, she sat up straighter. No, the love

she'd felt from him wasn't faked. That kiss sure wasn't fake. And she *was* stronger now. Wiser. Unsure as to why he'd pushed her away, Randi realized one thing...his tactic wouldn't work. He probably assumed she was the same person she'd been when he'd left. Not anymore—and hadn't been for a long time. She might hide from the world, but that didn't mean she couldn't stand on her own two feet and fight for what she wanted—fight for the *man* she wanted.

She had hauled him halfway through the forest with not much more than her sheer will power and she wasn't about to let the man push her away so easily. Agent Wade Malone would have to explain himself and give a darned good reason as to why he wanted nothing more to do with her because, in her heart and soul, she knew he loved her. Even if he hadn't said it out loud, she'd felt it in the way he'd held her, kissed her.

As steely determination lined her backbone, she stood and grinned. The man didn't know what was about to hit him.

****

Wade hated himself. There was a deep void in his heart where Miranda had been, where she had touched his soul and rekindled a fire he thought he'd ground out under the heel of his boot. But he didn't have time to think about what he'd done to her. Within minutes after she'd left, Agents' Wesson and Smith, along with the field supervisor, arrived to debrief him.

He learned the sheriff had found two locals who had been paid by Fry to show him a back way onto Miranda's property. For the time being, they were both residents of the county jail, charged with accessory. They were lucky, though. Men like Fry didn't leave witnesses...of any kind. Why he hadn't killed the two men before kidnapping Miranda was a miscalculation on his part.

Philip Fry's dead body had been retrieved from the pit and all the loose ends wrapped up. Thankfully, the other agents left shortly thereafter, leaving Wade his orders. After he was released from the hospital, he'd return to the Kansas City office...just like he'd told Miranda. Only this was official and not a reason to get her to leave. Pending his medical release, he'd be on desk duty until he was fit to go back out into the field. Normally, he hated desk duty and waiting for injuries to heal. This time, he simply didn't care. The only thing he thought about was leaving Miranda behind.

He visualized her home. There was a warmth within those walls that touched the core of his being, welcoming him. The pictures and art on the walls depicting Arkansas, her work room with the varied types of paintings, the cozy kitchen, the cat. He'd never liked cats before. A corner of his lip tilted upward at the memory of the ornery feline demanding attention. He'd miss that critter.

The smile slipped away and deep sadness settled over him. Logically, pushing Miranda away was the best thing. He scrubbed his face, the day-old beard scraping his palms.

One excuse after another popped into his mind as he tried to justify his actions. Then the object of his thoughts, the woman who made him whole, walked into the room. All reason blasted out the window.

She'd come back.

He worked to suppress the smile that lit up his heart as he drank in the sight of her. He felt as if he'd been in a desert the last nine years, and only she could quench his thirst. Desperately, he wanted to pull her into his arms and crush his lips to hers, to run his hands along the length of her body, memorizing every luscious inch of her, to spend the rest of his life with her. But he didn't have the right to do any of those things.

"Wade."

The sound of her voice drifted over him in a caress he didn't deserve. Her eyes were a bit puffy, as if she'd been crying. Tears he'd caused.

"I saved your sorry hyde last night, and if you think you can push me out of your life so easily, then you aren't as smart as some people think you are." She might look as if she'd been crying, but she didn't sound it. No, she was in complete control. And determined.

He swallowed. Hard. "Miranda, you don't know what you're saying."

"I know exactly what I'm saying...and what I'm feeling." She crossed her arms over her chest, staring him down.

He shook his head. "Being around me can be hazardous. Didn't last night teach you anything?"

"And that happens on a weekly basis?" She wasn't giving an inch.

"Well, not exactly. But my job is dangerous."

"Seriously? I hadn't noticed." He couldn't miss the sarcasm in her voice.

"I'd be gone a lot."

"And?"

What was wrong with her? None of his reasons phased her in the least. Who *was* this woman, and what happened to the girl he'd pledged his love to all those years ago?

"You know, Malone, there's more than one way for a relationship to work. All you have to do is find what works best for each couple. Not only do both parties have to compromise, but they each have to give 100% and put the other person first. Did you ever think of that?"

Unable to meet her steady gaze, he laid his head back against the pillow and stared at the ceiling. She needed to understand. This was for her own good, her own safety. So why did it feel so wrong to tell her goodbye? "I'm tired and need to rest." He rolled over and turned his back to her.

She didn't leave. In fact, she moved to the other side of the bed. "You aren't going to fake me out with that sleeping routine. I'm not leaving until I have answers."

Stubborn woman. Right now, Wade couldn't express how proud he was of her. He was alive because of her, pure and simple. To top it off, she wasn't backing down here, either. Giving in, he raised the bed. He wanted—no, needed—to see her face.

"I owe you an apology. The way I acted yesterday morning was inexcusable. Hell, I've pretty much acted like an ass since I got here."

She raised her eyebrows and pursed her lips at his comment. "You won't get any argument from me there."

Damn, this was going to be harder than he thought. Suddenly feeling shy, as if he were a teenager with a crush on the most popular girl in school, he asked, "You aren't going to make this easy for me, are you?"

She crossed her arms over her chest and slowly

shook her head. "Nope."

"You've got more guts than a lot of men I know. I admire your tenacity and the fact you stuck it out last night."

She lowered her gaze, and a full blush crept up her neck. "I just did what—"

"No. Most people give up to save their own skin. I've seen it too many times. But you didn't. That takes a lot of courage."

"Well, you could've distracted the kidnapper by telling him where I was, but you didn't"

"Wouldn't have done any good if I had. He was going to kill me regardless, then come looking for you. I never turn my back on my partner. And, apparently, neither do you. You saved my life."

He motioned her closer, then took her hands in his, loving the feel of her skin against his.

"I think you saved both our lives, and took care of the bad guy in the process." She smiled shyly.

He pulled her down, and as his lips met hers, he felt as if he had come home. A deep and profound peace settled over him. But things still needed to be said, and he reluctantly ended the kiss. She whimpered, but he was resolved to get the words out before he got lost in her.

"Miranda, you have to know, I won't do anything to disrupt our daughter's life."

She sucked in an audible breath. "Oh, Wade. That means so much! Thank you."

"It's killing me, but she's better off where she is. I'd like to see her, though. I know it'd be from afar, but—"

"It was an open adoption."

"—I. What?" Was he hearing correctly?

"You can meet Katie, Wade. In fact, I think she'd like that. She has asked a time or two about her father, but I didn't tell her much."

"Katie?"

She nodded, smiling. "Katie Marie."

"But her parents…"

"They're wonderful people. They'd welcome you. Trust me."

Speechless, all the things he wanted to say stuck in his throat. Her name was Katie and she wanted to meet him? And her parents didn't object? Love swelled in his heart. Hope bloomed.

He gazed deeply into Miranda's green eyes. Eyes brimming with tears. "You're a strong woman. I admire and respect you. I know I don't have any right to ask, and it isn't fair to impose my lifestyle on you, but woman, I can't go on breathing without you."

Deep in the depths of her gaze, he saw mischief, and love and…promise.

Sunshine burst through the window, chasing away all of his doubts and fears. For the last nine years he'd lived in the shadow of the love they'd professed to each other…of the pledge they'd both broken.

"Miranda, I promise to always be true to you, to care for you—and Sebastian—and to always be there for you. I don't know how we'll work this out, but there'll be time for details later." He mentally shook himself. That last part wasn't what he wanted to say at all! So instead of talking, he pulled her into a deep kiss that held all the love he could offer.

He finally broke the kiss, and with his arms still wrapped around her, he said, "My beautiful, sweet, strong Miranda. I love you and my heart is in your hands. Do you think there's any chance for us after all this time?"

Miranda didn't take her gaze from his. She leaned forward, and a breath away from his lips, she whispered, "I'm not going anywhere. I'm not leaving this hospital room. I'm not leaving your side. You're stuck with me, Malone. Forever and a day and beyond."

Wade smiled. He was where he was always meant to be. There'd be no more shattered promises...in either of their lives.

A word about the author...

An Award-Winning and Amazon Kindle sales top 25 Bestselling author, Oklahoma native Linda Trout loves Happily-Ever-Afters. She counts herself lucky to having grown up in a small farming town with small town values. Getting lost in a good book is one of her favorite pastimes so it was natural that she turned to writing, wanting to create intriguing stories of her own. Between her numerous cats, who think they have to help her write, and traveling to various parts of the country, she's working on her next novel. http://LindaTrout.com

CPSIA information can be obtained
at www.ICGtesting.com
Printed in the USA
LVHW020520280922
729418LV00012B/507